Don't Drink the Water

A Comedy in Two Acts

by Woody Allen

A SAMUEL FRENCH ACTING EDIT

SAMUEL FRENCH

FOUNDED 1830

New York Hollywood London Toronto

SAMUELFRENCH.COM

DON'T DRINK THE WATER, by Woody Allen, produced by David Merrick in association with Jack Rollins and Charles Joffe, directed by Stanley Prager, was presented at the Morosco Theatre, N.Y.C., Nov. 17, 1966.

CHARACTERS
(*In Order of Their Appearance*)

FATHER DROBNEY	*Dick Libertini*
AMBASSABOR MAGEE	*House Jameson*
KILROY	*Gerry Matthews*
AXEL MAGEE	*Anthony Roberts*
MARION HOLLANDER	*Kay Medford*
WALTER HOLLANDER	*Lou Jacobi*
SUSAN HOLLANDER	*Anita Gillette*
KROJACK	*James Dukas*
BURNS	*Curtis Wheeler*
CHEF	*Gene Varrone*
SULTAN OF BASHIR	*Oliver Clark*
SULTAN'S FIRST WIFE	*Donna Mills*
KASNAR	*John Hallow*
COUNTESS BORDONI	*Sharon Talbot*
NOVOTNY	*Luke Andreas*
WALTER	*Jonathan Bolt*

SYNOPSIS OF SCENES

The action of the play takes place in an American Embassy somewhere behind the Iron Curtain.

ACT ONE

SCENE 1: A late summer afternoon
SCENE 2: Later the same day
SCENE 3: Several days later
SCENE 4: Late that night
SCENE 5: Several days later

3

ACT TWO

Don't Drink the Water

ACT ONE

Scene 1

Before Rise: *The HOUSE LIGHTS dim and we hear what sounds like the national ANTHEM of some Middle European country. Very martial and pompous and official. After a chorus of it, it SPEEDS up to the wrong speed and sounds rickey-tick.*

Scene: *The HOUSE LIGHTS go out and the CURTAIN rises on the American Embassy in a small, Iron Curtain country somewhere in Eastern Europe. It is a very small but very quaint, charming, old-world little mansion that is done in the best of elegance. The walls are beautifully wood panelled and mirrored. The chandeliers are beautiful. Upstage there are two large doors. The one u.l. leads to the staircase upstairs which is visible. The one u.r. leads to the front doors which are not. Presumably one enters, is greeted in a receiving area by a gentleman who sits out at a desk there, and is given directions to any of several rooms depending on his business. The room we are concerned with is, for want of a better term, the main room. There are other rooms, such as a tiny auditorium on floor two with a large, dominating portrait of the President of the United States, and also several minor rooms on the first floor that are used for filing, a small business office for the ambassador and one for his assistant and probably a small, tastefully done smoking room or conference room, but this is the nucleus of the place. Here,*

5

dignitaries discuss, chat, have drinks, plans are laid, negotiations felt out, and when small parties or receptions are held, this is the main room although guests spill out into other parts of the building. It is furnished with that sparse elegance that one might find in one of the rooms in the White House like the Blue Room or the Red Room. Small areas for conversation here and there, perhaps for tea or brandy, a prim sofa, a small leather top desk with phone that is quite antique and beautiful magnificent wood floors smartly waxed and maybe one lovely area rug contribute to a simple but rich looking room. U.L. *there is a lovely porcelain tile stove. There are open doors at* L. *and* R., *for this room, because of its central location, is a main artery leading to its adjoining rooms, just the barest bits of which we might be able to glimpse, one of them being a much smaller, but beautifully done, office of the ambassador, and on the other side, perhaps a lovely hallway that would eventually lead to some other small rooms. In this room in addition to a mirror on the wall and some very simple American landscapes, there might be a portrait of the President or the Official Seal.*

TIME: *The present.*

AT RISE: *The Stage is empty. From down the Upstage staircase comes the spectre-like tall, emaciated, cassocked figure of* FATHER DROBNEY, *a priest who speaks with an accent. He faces the audience and one can detect behind his eyes the faint glimmer of an eccentric.*

DROBNEY. (*Crosses* D.L.C.) Good evening. My name is Drobney. Father Drobney. I am a priest in this charming little Communist country where out of four million inhabitants, 3,975,000 are atheists, and about 24,000 are agnostics—and the other thousand are Jewish. The point is: I don't have a big following. This is the United States Embassy of this country. Six years ago I ran in here seeking asylum from the Communist police. Outside these walls were four million Communists determined to kill me! My choice was simple. I could remain here in the safety of your embassy, or I could go outside and attempt the biggest mass conversion in history. I decided to stay and I've been hiding upstairs ever since. The head of this Embassy is Ambassador James F. Magee. He was put in charge here by your government because of his firm grasp of world events. (*Enter* AMBASSADOR MAGEE, *hard-nosed, dignified in his mid-fifties, a career-organization-team man. He goes* R. *to window and looks out*.) Each morning for the past four years he enters this room, surveys the environment, and graces us with his clarity and wisdom.

AMBASSADOR. Jesus, look at all those Communists!

DROBNEY. This is typical of his ability to sum up a situation brilliantly. (AMBASSADOR MAGEE *goes to desk and loads briefcase with papers for a trip.* KILROY *enters* R. *with pad and pencil, poised at the* AMBASSADOR'S *side.* KILROY *is a punctilious rat and you can smell his type a mile away*.) Mr. Kilroy is Ambassador Magee's bright-eyed efficient assistant.

KILROY. (*Out front*.) I am the only man in the Foreign Service who knows the words to the second stanza of the Star Spangled Banner.

DROBNEY. All of his vital memos are sent through Mr. Kilroy.

AMBASSADOR. Mr. Kilroy, take a vital memo: To all Embassy personnel: Unless a new embassy building is purchased, we must think of new ways to make room in this small mansion. It was unfortunate that when Dean Rusk passed through the country last week we were unable to put him up for the night. It was equally unfortunate that no one here recognized him. See this does not happen again.

(KILROY *exits smartly*, R. *Enter* AXEL MAGEE, L., *about*

*28, a pleasant well-meaning young man whose career
in the foreign service has been a series of disasters.
He is always trying but somehow everything always
manages to go wrong for him. Crosses to the Am-
BASSADOR.*)

DROBNEY. And this is Ambassador Magee's other assistant. Not exactly bright-eyed, not exactly efficient, in
fact the only man in the history of the foreign service to
accidentally wrap his lunch in a peace treaty.

MAGEE. (*Out front.*) I've worked in seventeen U.S.
embassies. Some for as long as three weeks.

DROBNEY. This young man has worked at this Embassy
for six months. That's the longest he's ever worked at any
one Embassy. Why? Because he's pleasant, he's eager
and he's the Ambassador's son.

MAGEE. You sent for me, Dad?

DROBNEY. And here is where it all starts. I better get
back to my room. (*Exits upstairs.*)

AMBASSADOR. (*Crosses to* D.L.C.) Axel, because of my
superior record here, the leaders of my party would like
to discuss the possibility of placing my name in the coming Gubernatorial race in our state.

MAGEE. Dad, I think you'd make a wonderful governor.
Your broad outlook would appeal to psychotic liberals as
well as militant fascists. Something for everyone.

AMBASSADOR. Naturally, in my absence this Embassy
must be run with the same brilliant efficiency it is ac-
customed to when I am here.

MAGEE. This is a quiet little outpost. There should be
no trouble.

AMBASSADOR. (*Crosses below* MAGEE.) I'll level with
you, Axel. I'm tempted to leave Mr. Kilroy in charge but
it looks bad for the family image.

MAGEE. Dad, the foreign service is my whole life. Give
me a chance to prove myself once and for all. What can
go wrong in two weeks?

AMBASSADOR. You were in Brazil for two weeks and you had them importing coffee!

MAGEE. Dad, I know how much that governorship means to you and I'll see that this Embassy remains a credit to your record.

AMBASSADOR. The only important guest we're going to have in the next two weeks is the Sultan of Bashir.

MAGEE. I'll see that the Sultan gets royal treatment.

AMBASSADOR. You sure will, Axel. I'm on the verge of concluding an oil deal with the Sultan that will make me a very big man next November. Axel, most fathers start their sons in the mail room and let them work their way up. I started you on top and you worked your way to the mail room. This Embassy is a clean start for you. If it's not run letter perfect, (*He crosses Up to arch.* MAGEE *crosses to desk.*) I'll fire you and if your own father fires you—it's the end of the line. Goodbye. (*Exits U.R., closes doors.*)

MAGEE. Have a good flight, Dad. (*Looks around, crosses and adjusts emblem, then straightens up confidently, croses to R. door and calls.*) Mr. Kilroy!

KILROY. (*Entering R. and crossing D.R. to desk.*) You called?

MAGEE. For the next two weeks I am in charge of this Embassy. Business will go on as usual and it would mean a great deal to me to have your full cooperation.

KILROY. (*Crosses D.L. to sofa.*) Your father should have known better than to leave in charge a man who was asked to leave Africa.

MAGEE. (*Crosses D.S. to desk.*) That's not fair. Some of the best men in the foreign service have at one time or another been recalled from a country.

KILROY. Africa is a continent. You've been recalled from an entire continent. And what about Japan, you never mention that, or the Soviet Union—you managed to cover that up, too.

MAGEE. (*Crosses to* KILROY.) You know I've had some bad breaks careerwise.

KILROY. (*Accusatory.*) And you were hung in effigy in Panama!

MAGEE. I admitted I was!

KILROY. Yes, but you didn't say it was by our own Embassy!

(*PHONE rings. They* BOTH *go for it.* KILROY *then realizes who's in charge and let's* MAGEE *get it.*)

MAGEE. (*Into phone.*) Yes? Yes, this is the American Embassy . . . Oh, no, Ambassador Magee is not here. He's on his way back to the United States. This is Axel Magee. I'm in charge during his absence. (*Sound of two GUNSHOTS just outside the embassy.*) What the hell is that all about? (*Slams down phone.*)

KILROY. (*Goes to window and* MAGEE *follows.*) It's the Communist police! They're chasing three people, they look like tourists. Mr. Magee, they're running up the steps of the Embassy!

MAGEE. (*Crosses* U.R. *to arch.*) We better open the front door quickly!

(MAGEE *runs and opens doors and in burst* MR. *and* MRS. WALTER HOLLANDER *and their daughter* SUSAN. *He is a typical tourist with loud short-sleeved shirt worn outside his pants and carries a camera. He wears a green hat. His wife carries a TWA bag. The* HOL-LANDERS *are a family from Newark on vacation. They are in their early fifties and despite their comical appearance, have a beautiful daughter of about 21. But we will come to that. Right now they are in a state of hysterical panic and fear.*)

MARION. Help! We are American tourists! The communists are after us! They think we're spies!

(*Two GUNSHOTS ring out.*)

WALTER. We're Americans! I swear! Willie Mays! Her-

shey Bars! (*Crosses to* MAGEE.) Kate Smith! I pledge
allegiance to the flag!

MARION. (*Crossing to* MAGEE.) And to the republic
for which it stands!

(*Two more GUNSHOTS.*)

SUSAN. It's the Communist police!
WALTER. Some vacation. Run!

(*The* HOLLANDERS *run off* U.L., SUSAN *separating from
her parents and heading up and off.* WALTER *and*
MARION *hide in an adjacent office* L. *An armed Communist* GUARD *races on* U.R., *crosses to* U.L. *arch,
followed quickly by* KROJACK, *menacing and vicious
head of the Secret Police. He wears a business suit
and carries an automatic.*)

KROJACK. (*Crossing to* MAGEE.) Where are they? Hand
them over to us.

MAGEE. Who? What? What did they do?

KROJACK. (*Booming.*) They were caught in the act of
spying!

MAGEE. How?

KROJACK. They were taking pictures in a restricted
area. (*The* GUARD *holds fast at arch and waits orders.*)

MAGEE. That doesn't make them spies. They're American tourists—didn't you see the shirt that guy was
wearing? What did they take pictures of?

KROJACK. Missile sites and rocket installations . . .
They have seen too much, they must die.

BURNS. (*Bursting in, frightened,* R. *crossing* U.L. *to
sofa.*) Mr. Magee, they're setting up searchlights and
machine guns around the embassy.

(*SEARCHLIGHT in window.*)

MAGEE. (*To* KROJACK.) I'm sure they didn't realize—

Look, I'll give you the film. In fact, I'll give you the whole camera.

KROJACK. (*Viciously.*) Hand them over to us or we will drag them out and shoot them!

MAGEE. (*Taking a stand.*) This Embassy is United States territory. Nobody can be dragged out of here and shot without the written consent of the American government.

KILROY. (*Crossing to* KROJACK.) Leave these premises at once. Your behavior is in extreme violation of international conduct.

KROJACK. (*Looks at* KILROY, *then at* MAGEE.) Who are you?

MAGEE. I'm Axel Magee. I am in charge of this Embassy in my father's absence and I order you to leave at once. Guns or no guns—if you don't go, Mr Kilroy will throw you out.

(*The* CHEF, *a temperamental eccentric, enters in a tizzy* U.L.)

CHEF. (*Crosses to* MAGEE.) Mr. Magee—something is happening!

MAGEE. Yes, Hatami, I know—

CHEF. There are soldiers surrounding the house. They are staring into the kitchen!

MAGEE. They won't hurt you.

CHEF. (*Suddenly an artist.*) I can't cook if I'm being stared at. I'm that kind of person.

KROJACK. Who are you?

CHEF. I am personal chef to Ambassador Magee, formerly chef to the King of Norway—formerly chef at the White House—formerly chef to the Queen of England . . . before that I did very little cooking.

MAGEE. Don't you terrorize our help!

CHEF. (*With bravado.*) I had a cake in the oven! Your gunshots made it fall! (*Exits in high dudgeon* U.L.)

KILROY. Mr. Magee, stand firm—I'll lodge a formal protest. (*Exits* R.)

MAGEE. (*Crosses to* R.C.) *You* stand firm, *I'll* . . . lodge . . . (*Now* MAGEE *is alone facing the guns.*) Look —you spy on us—we spy on you—everybody knows it. Why do we suddenly pretend it's so unusual?

KROJACK. (*Seizes on this, crossing to him.*) You do spy on us?

MAGEE. Huh?

KROJACK. (*It interests him.*) How often?

MAGEE. (*Trying to calm things down.*) All the time. It's no secret. (*Crosses to* C.) Espionage goes on between our countries every day. Why be so hypocritical about it?

KROJACK. It does, huh? And are *they* spies?

MAGEE. No—maybe—I don't know—

KROJACK. How do you know they're not spies? You never saw them before?

MAGEE. Are you going to tell me your country doesn't send spies into the United States posing as tourists?

KROJACK. (*Crossing to him; pressing him.*) Then you admit they're spies?

MAGEE. (*Just trying to be civilized.*) What if they are? That doesn't give you the right to enter this building illegally. You're going to start an international incident. This is not just an outrage but a vicious and cruel attack on the whole free world. I wouldn't be surprised if France took our side.

KILROY. (*Enters* R., *crosses* D.R. *to* KROJACK.) Mr. Krojack—I have your foreign affairs office on the phone. They want you to report back immediately.

KROJACK. He admitted they are spies.

KILROY. (*Stunned.*) You didn't, Mr. Magee!

MAGEE. (*A step to* L.) Ah, well, er . . . ah—

KROJACK. He admitted it. I have it all here on tape. (*Produces miniature tape recorder from his pocket.*)

MAGEE. (*Crosses to* KILROY.) I did—in a sense—Mr. Kilroy—you know, we spy—they spy—

KILROY. (*Crosses below* MAGEE *to* KROJACK. *Yelling into tape recorder.*) We do nothing of the sort.

MAGEE. (*Still trying and making things worse.*) Actually we do—if we all stop being hypocritical and be honest for once—

KILROY. (*Turning on him.*) That's enough. Mr. Magee!

MAGEE. We do spy—

KROJACK. (*Extends tape recorder.*) Will you speak louder, please.

MAGEE. (*Crosses to sofa.*) Now, look, don't twist my words. You come barging in here with guns—then you wonder why a brutal dictatorship gets a bad name! . . .

KROJACK. The Embassy will be surrounded from this day on. The spies will either come out—or spend the rest of their lives in here. But first the *world* will hear this confession. Goodbye for now. (*Motions* GUARD *to come. They exit* U.R.)

KILROY. (*Crosses* C.) How could you do it? How could you admit they were spies?

MAGEE. (*Crosses below* KILROY *to* D.L.C.) I panicked—I lost control.

KILROY. What were you thinking?

MAGEE. I was thinking—don't panic! Don't lose control!

WALTER. (*Enters with* MARION *from* L. *Crossing to* MAGEE.) You!

MAGEE. Who?

WALTER. Yeah! You with the vest. Why did you tell them we're spies?

MARION. Walter—be careful. He's always eavesdropping.

WALTER. How could you tell them we're spies? They say we're spies—he tells 'em yes. All of a sudden I'm a spy. I'll go on "What's My Line"—they'll never guess.

MARION. Where's my daughter?

KILROY. (*Crosses to* R. *door.*) I'll get her. (*Calling.*) Mr. Burns. Bring the girl up from the basement.

MAGEE. Yes, (*Calling.*) Mr. Burns—bring the girl up from the basement.

WALTER. What are you—his echo?

MARION. Walter, be quiet.

WALTER. Those lunatics out there accuse us of spying and this lunatic says yes.

MAGEE. If you were listening to the conversation you should know that I was trying to calm them down.

MARION. First no movie on the plane—then this.

MAGEE. It's a simple misunderstanding.

MARION. How simple?

WALTER. (*To* MARION.) If we leave the building they kill us. Simple enough?

MAGEE. Don't jump to conclusions. There'd be a trial first. (*He stepped in it again.*)

WALTER. Who is this guy?

KILROY. (*Crosses* U.L. *to sofa.*) I'd better call your father. Maybe I can stop him at the airport. (*Goes toward next office.*)

MAGEE. (*Crosses to* KILROY.) There's no need for that. I can handle a crisis. (*Wants to stop him.*)

KILROY. Handle one? You are one. (*Exits* R.)

WALTER. (*Crosses to sofa.*) A man takes his family on vacation—he wants to show them a good time—this is what we have working in our government. Then they wonder why I don't vote.

MAGEE. (*Crosses to desk.*) I've got to make out a report. (*Clumsily seizing all manner of loose forms in triplicate from the desk.*)

MARION. (*Crosses to* WALTER.) Well, that's what you get for taking pictures.

WALTER. It's my vacation. My new hobby is photography. Am I interested in their missiles and rockets? All I want to do is take some pictures.

MAGEE. (*Crosses to* MARION.) I wonder if your photos are valuable?

MARION. He held the camera backwards. They're pictures of his nose.

WALTER. I gotta have my head examined. Every time I listen to you I wind up behind the eight ball.

MARION. Here we go again.

WALTER. If you had listened to me, we would've taken a cabana in Atlantic Beach.

MARION. Every year it must be Atlantic Beach. What's the matter—they need you to work the tide?

WALTER. (*Crosses to* D.L.C.) No, we had to go to Europe. Thirty-five hundred dollars for three weeks of uninterrupted diarrhea.

MARION. What's so terrible? My brother suggested we see Europe. He had a wonderful time here.

WALTER. I'm tired of living for your brother. (*To* MAGEE.) I have to run my life by her brother. That's a hot one.

MAGEE. (*A step* D.R.) I realize you're upset—if I could just get some facts . . .

MARION. Mr. and Mrs. Walter Hollander—Newark, New Jersey.

WALTER. You want to know the facts? (MAGEE *crosses Up*.) The facts are I have a three-week vacation. I said, let's take a cabana at Atlantic Beach—there's sun—you can play pinochle—there's miniature golf. No, her brother says—go to Europe. (*Crosses to* L.C. *chair*.) And behind the Iron Curtain no less. I needed this like a growth. (*He sits*.)

MARION. (*Crosses to* WALTER.) Aren't you interested in how the other half lives? We went with you to the Folies Bergere in Paris.

WALTER. Are you comparing Communism to those girls?

MARION. (*To* MAGEE.) As if he appreciates Europe any place. We took him to Westminster Abbey—his feet hurt. We took him to St. Peter's in Rome—he got dizzy from looking up. We took him to the Louve—I hate to tell you what happened.

WALTER. (*Rises*.) It's pronounced Louv-re—Louv-re—that's how much you know.

MARION. (*Crosses to* D.R.C.) In the Louv-re he struck a match across a Van Gogh. I thought I'd die.

MAGEE. (*Trying to fill out forms*.) Have either of you

two ever had any respiratory ailments—? (*Crosses up to desk.*) Oh, wrong forms—

MARION. (*Crosses to* R. *of desk. To* MAGEE.) I have a brother, see? He's a wonderful man.

WALTER. (*Crosses to* L. *of desk.*) He's a Nazi.

MARION. Do you know what you're talking about?

WALTER. (*To* MAGEE.) Take my word for it—he should be wearing an armband.

MAGEE. (*Crosses to* D.R. *of desk. Trying to get correct form.*) Here we are—seeking asylum.

WALTER. (*Crosses to* MAGEE.) I'm not seeking asylum—I didn't do anything. I'm a caterer from New Jersey.

MAGEE. I'll need your passports and I have to get some information.

MARION. I'm giving you information. It began with my brother—quite a lovely individual.

WALTER. They should have hung him at Nuremberg.

MAGEE. (*Consulting form.*) Have you ever bought anything on credit? (*Realizes it's wrong again. Runs to desk to get more.*)

MARION. My brother went to Europe last year. He had a wonderful time. He suggested we bring my daughter—it's cultural. My brother is an intellectual.

WALTER. (*Crosses* D.L.C.) Some intellectual—like Sonny Liston.

MAGEE. (*Crosses to* WALTER.) And you're just a caterer. Nobody paid you to take pictures of anything or anything like that . . .

WALTER. (*Hands him a card.*) Hollander and Blackwell—finest in Newark. Here's my card.

MAGEE. Do you work, Mrs. Hollander?

MARION. No, sir—I'm an average housewife.

WALTER. Some housewife. She's a professional mah-jongg hustler. She carries around her own tiles.

MAGEE. And you accidentally wandered into a restricted area. I mean, you didn't sneak in or anything . . .

MARION. I told him it looked like private property,

but he had to get a photograph. He said "Why? 'Cause there's guards and dogs and barbed wire?" I said "Yes, 'cause there's guards and dogs and barbed wire." (*Turning on* WALTER.) What did you think it was—a place that sold guards and dogs and barbed wire?

MAGEE. Then they chased you and you had the good sense to come here?

MARION. My daughter had the presence of mind.

MAGEE. She did the right thing, Mrs. Hollander.

WALTER. Sure—so you could tell them we're spies. My wife should not have to go through this. She's not a young woman.

(MARION *reacts surprised*.)

MAGEE. On the one hand we want to protect you—on the other hand we want to protect the best interests of the United States.

WALTER. I always thought they went hand in hand.

MARION. I'm an old woman?

WALTER. (*Crossing to her. Affectionately*.) I didn't mean old. I meant young-old. (*Kisses her*.)

MAGEE. (*Crosses to* WALTER.) There's nothing to worry about.

WALTER. Sure, because I'm a caterer—not a spy. Creative catering—our specialty. We were the first to make bridegrooms out of potato salad.

MARION. He does lovely work, I'll say that for him.

WALTER. Last month we did a wedding reception. (*Crosses* D.L.C.) We did the bride's body in jello—her head in a very nice clam dip—with fruit punch spouting out of her throat. It was a class affair.

MAGEE. I should have this settled in a few days.

WALTER. What do you mean? What do you think I'm gonna do—live here?

MAGEE. It may require some effort, but we're going to show those communists their police state tactics don't work. I'll have Mr. Kilroy see if we have some spare cots.

WALTER. Cots? I will not sleep on a cot. I'm a dignified human being with a hernia.

MAGEE. It's an emergency, Mr. Hollander, and we'll try our best.

WALTER. (*Crosses below* MARION *to* MAGEE.) I got a business. Sam Blackwell can't run the firm. He's the inside man. I'm the outside man. It requires personality.

KILROY. (*Entering abruptly* R. *and crosses to* MAGEE.) Mr. Hollander, was there some kind of a notebook in your suitcase back in the hotel—with some kind of party list in it?

WALTER. (*Crosses to him.*) No. Oh, yes. The Levine wedding estimate.

KILROY. What is that?

WALTER. The Levine wedding—how many from the bride's side—how many from the groom's side—how much roast beef—how much grapefruit.

KILROY. The communist police say they've been working on it and they've broken the code.

WALTER. What code?

KILROY. Supply information and troop movements.

WALTER. Troop movements? That's the Levines and the Wassermans. There's more Levines because she's paying for the wedding and they eat like an army, but they're civilians.

MAGEE. It's that damn Krojack trying to frame you.

WALTER. (*Crosses to* MARION.) I can't stay here. This is the height of the season. I got weddings coming up, I got receptions, I got coming-out parties. Sam Blackwell can't handle it by himself. He lacks my charm.

MARION. So he'll have his son come in and help out. He's over twenty-one.

WALTER. His son? Who's gonna dress him?

MAGEE. Your business can manage for a few days.

WALTER. You think so? And, now, if you'll excuse me, I'm going to America. Where's my hat? (*Starts toward door*)

MARION. Mr. Magee, what do you think's going to happen?

WALTER. Let them capture me. I'm a caterer.

KILROY. This is preposterous. (*Exits* R.)

WALTER. They want information? I'll tell them how to make grapefruit sections. (*It looks like he may try to leave.*)

MAGEE. Mr. Hollander, you can't go out there.

MARION. (*Crossing* L.C. *to chair. Calling his bluff.*) Let him go out there. Go ahead, big shot. We'll be in here if you want us. Go ahead. There's the front door.

MAGEE. (*Caught in the middle.*) Now, look—

WALTER. (*Crosses to* C. *To* MARION.) Don't think I won't.

MARION. Go ahead. Stop talking already and do it.

MAGEE. Mrs. Hollander, don't start trouble.

WALTER. You think I'm afraid of those guys?

MARION. No. Why should you be afraid? They're only secret police. They'll arrest you and torture you. What's to be afraid of?

WALTER. (*Crossing to* MARION.) You think I'm afraid to walk out?

MARION. No—go ahead—get brainwashed—in your case it'll probably help.

MAGEE. I strongly urge you not to do anything rash—

MARION. Let him go—go ahead—go.

WALTER. (*He gets to door, pauses, comes quickly back to* MAGEE.) Do you know if any of those guys belong to the Masons?

(MARION *waves her hand at him as if to say she knew he was bluffing.*)

SUSAN. (*Enter* U.L., *led by* BURNS, *who continues off. Crosses to* MARION.) I've been hiding down in the basement.

MARION. Mr. Magee, this is my daughter Susan. She was a Caesarian.

SUSAN. How do you do, Mr. Magee?

MAGEE. (*Obviously taken with her looks. She is an offbeat Villagey-looking girl but a stunner.*) A—Axel Magee—

SUSAN. Are we free to go home yet?

MAGEE. (*A little tongue-tied.*) Home?

WALTER. Sure we're free to go home. Did you see what's doing out there, thanks to this guy? We're liable to be stuck here three, four days.

MAGEE. (*To* SUSAN.) I'm awfully sorry for this inconvenience. I realize it's terrible—

SUSAN. I think it's fun.

MAGEE. (*Delighted at her attitude.*) It can be fun. Some people might look upon this as an exciting experience.

WALTER. Some people bought Edsels.

SUSAN. (*To her* FATHER, *crossing toward him.*) We could be worse off. This place is lovely.

WALTER. And what are we supposed to do about Seth?

MARION. Seth? Oh my God!

WALTER. Forgive her. In her panic she's completely forgotten that she gave birth twice.

MARION. I wasn't even worried about Seth. He's at camp.

WALTER. (*Crosses to* MARION.) Camp ends tomorrow. If we're not back to let him in, what's going to happen? He'll be unsupervised. He'll live in the streets. He'll run amuck. He'll rape and loot. You know our son. He takes after your brother.

MARION. (*Crosses to* SUSAN.) I just thought of something. Susan's getting married next week.

WALTER. That's right. I have a deposit on the hall.

MAGEE. (*Obviously disappointed.*) Getting married, huh? (*A step in.*) I guess you're really anxious to get out of here.

SUSAN. That's a long story, Mr. Magee.

WALTER. Let's not discuss it. The date's been set.

MARION. (*Crosses to* WALTER.) Well, we may have to

push the date back—so you better call the owner of the Renaissance Luau and get our deposit back.

WALTER. (*To* SUSAN.) You better call Donald. He'll be worried sick.

SUSAN. I'll call. Mr. Magee, what's the longest anyone has ever had to stay here?

MAGEE. (*Uncomfortably.*) Er—we gave asylum to a priest who's been living upstairs—er—a while.

WALTER. What's a while?

MAGEE. Oh, er—you know—a while—

MARION. How long?

MAGEE. (*After a lot of squirming.*) Six years.

WALTER. (*Dumbstruck.*) Six years? I said, let's go to Atlantic Beach—we'll swim—we'll play pinochle—no, her brother says—go to Europe—may he rest in peace . . .

MARION. He's not dead.

WALTER. He should *be!*

BLACKOUT

ACT ONE

SCENE 2

Later that night. MAGEE *is seated at desk.* KILROY *and* BURNS *are lugging a cot across the room.* ALL *are pretty beat.*

KILROY. Oh . . . you could at least give us a hand, Mr. Magee.

MAGEE. (*Rises.*) Look, Mr. Kilroy. I've been on the phone for the past six hours with Washington, with their Embassy, with the U.N. The whole picture has become clear to me now.

KILROY. What whole picture?

MAGEE. (*Crosses* D.R. *of desk.*) It's all over the American press. This morning the FBI captured this country's top secret agent. Adolph Lopert. The Grey Fox.

KILROY. (*Setting cot down.*) The Grey Fox?

MAGEE. One of their most brilliant spies. They caught him posing as a student at Berkeley. Apparently the Reds went after the first American tourists they could find, in retaliation.

KILROY. Now I suppose they want to trade spies. Adolph Lopert for the Hollanders.

MAGEE. Washington won't hear of it. They're outraged.

KILROY. I wonder if that's the way it's going to be from now on. Everytime we arrest one of their spies, they arrest one of our caterers.

BURNS. I better help the chef. Mr. Hollander is driving him crazy. He hates European food.

KILROY. (*Crosses to* MAGEE.) Mr. Magee, are you aware that the Sultan of Bashir is due here Friday? I suggest we postpone it for a more auspicious moment.

MAGEE. Nonsense, Mr. Kilroy. I should have this cleared up by Friday.

KILROY. And if you don't?

MAGEE. If I don't, business will go on as usual. *I'm* running this embassy.

SUSAN. (*Enters* L. *and crosses* D.S. *of table.*) Oh, Mr. Magee, may I please speak with you?

MAGEE. (*Crosses to* SUSAN.) Certainly. Mr. Kilroy, please. I'm sorry about your accommodations but we are jammed and it is temporary.

(BURNS *and* KILROY *carry cot off* L.)

SUSAN. Mr. Magee—I hope you're not upset by my parents.

MAGEE. Upset?

SUSAN. They're really sweet people—they just have their own way of expressing themselves. Don't let their form of communication throw you—

MAGEE. Listen, you don't have to explain parents to me. I have two parents. I *had* two parents. (*Crosses* D.C.) My mother is in court trying to disown me.

SUSAN. (*Crosses toward him.*) Mr. Kilroy explained to us that your father is Ambassador Magee.

MAGEE. Did he also tell you if I don't make it here I'm finished?

SUSAN. Oh. It's not that bad. Everybody makes mistakes. Everytime I pick up the papers I read about another diplomatic crisis cropping up somewhere in the world.

MAGEE. Have you noticed my name is in every article?

SUSAN. Funny. You're just the opposite of Donald.

MAGEE. Who's Donald?

SUSAN. He's my fiance. He's so confident and totally in command.

MAGEE. (*Crosses to sofa.*) Well, I'm confident too. Between major international blunders.

SUSAN. (*Crosses toward him.*) Well, I don't know about anybody else, but I'm beginning to like it here.

MAGEE. Gee, it's awfully sweet of you to take that attitude—I really appreciate it.

SUSAN. I mean it. It's very exciting and romantic. Most people spend their whole lives without anything like this happening to them.

MAGEE. So your father keeps telling me.

SUSAN. Danger stimulates me. You know how many babies were born in England in World War II as a result of the blitz?

MAGEE. —Well, if it's danger you want—take a look out there—must be two dozen professional killers. (*Gesturing outside the window.* SUSAN *crosses above sofa to window.*)

SUSAN. (*Looking.*) It's hard to see much . . .

MAGEE. (*Crosses to light.*) Here—knock off that light —you'll be able to see all the guards and secret police . . . (*He turns off the LIGHT; the MOONLIGHT comes through the window.*)

SUSAN. Oh sure—look at them out there—they've got machine guns . . . Are you married, Mr. Magee?

MAGEE. One thing about my work—you don't usually get to meet any attractive American women.

SUSAN. (*Crosses to* D.R. *sofa and sits.*) Oh?—don't you have a girl friend—or someone back home?

MAGEE. (*Crosses to sofa and sits.*) Actually, my work has caused me to travel a lot. Suddenly. What do you do? Are you a model or an actress or something?

SUSAN. No. I danced. In the New York City Center Ballet. And I was a folk singer and I worked in a coffee house in Greenwich Village.

MAGEE. Waitress?

SUSAN. I repaired motorcycles. Right now my big interest is painting.

MAGEE. No kidding—I paint. You'd hate my work though—it's all very abstract—I stand back and splash oil all over everything and then I run all over it with my sneakers and I stick my lunch on it—in fact, my lunch came in second at a showing in Cape Cod.

SUSAN. I adore abstract art.

MAGEE. Really. I'm a big Jackson Pollack man. His drippings best express my mental state. After dinner if you're interested, I'll show you a little statue I made out of some old automobile parts and a bedpan.

SUSAN. I'd love it.

MAGEE. (*Coming close to her and intimate.*) Y'know, you're really very pretty.

SUSAN. Thank you.

CHEF. (*Enters, agitated,* U.L. *and crosses* D.C.) Forgive my intrusion, Mr. Magee, but I must know what is the decision for dinner.

MAGEE. (*Rises.*) What's the problem? (*Crossing and turning on LIGHT.*)

CHEF. It's him.

MAGEE. Who?

CHEF. Mr. Hollander.

SUSAN. (*Rises. To* MAGEE.) Be nice to him. I'll see you at dinner. (*Goes upstairs.*)

CHEF. Every dish I name he says no.

MAGEE. Does he have any suggestion?

CHEF. Mr. Magee—we are four thousand miles from the United States, this is a Communist country, it's eight o'clock at night—where do you expect me to get Sara Lee coffee cake?

WALTER. (*Enters angrily* U.L. *and crosses to* L.C. *chair and sits.*) What kind of place is this?

CHEF. (*Running to him.*) Oysters.

WALTER. I will not eat oysters. They're alive when you eat them. I want my food dead—not sick, not wounded —dead.

CHEF. It's too late now to get anything new—take a very nice piece of veal.

WALTER. You must be joking.

CHEF. What's wrong with veal? My recipe is one of the great secrets of European cooking.

WALTER. Really? Let's keep it that way.

CHEF. (*Appealing.*) Mr. Magee. I have very little. If I had known. I couldn't get to the market—there were soldiers outside—

MAGEE. Try and understand, Mr. Hollander, our menu here is particularly elaborate because we entertain guests from all over the world.

WALTER. (*Rises.*) All I want is a plain piece of boiled chicken.

MARION. (*Enters* U.L. *and crosses to* WALTER.) Walter, where did you go off to?

WALTER. You know I can't get a meal here.

MARION. I'll come in the kitchen and make you something.

WALTER. Good.

CHEF. Madam. How do you live with this man? Do you force-feed him?

MARION. Don't worry. I know what he likes.

CHEF. (*Getting hysterical.*) I warn you, Madam, no one has ever been in my kitchen before. If you do anything to spoil the order of my spice rack, I don't know

what I'll do. Do you hear me? I don't know what I'll do!
(*Storms out in a rage,* U.L.)

WALTER. It's good to know our food is being cooked by an outpatient.

MARION. I spoke to Barney Silverman on the phone.

WALTER. Did you tell him not to drive to Newark Airport with the station wagon because we may be six years late?

MAGEE. (*Crosses to* MARION.) Mrs. Hollander—I wanted to speak to you about the phone. Naturally you're free to use it . . . if you could limit yours calls to a few dozen.

WALTER. (*Crosses to* L. *chair.*) This is nothing for her. She has to alert everyone in Newark, individually, like Paul Revere. (*Sits.*)

MARION. I called the Kleins and they'll take care of Seth till we get back.

WALTER. You couldn't find a worse couple?

MARION. (*Crosses to* WALTER.) What's wrong with the Kleins?

WALTER. They have orgies.

MARION. How do you know?

WALTER. I catered one.

SUSAN. (*Enters* U.L., *bringing with her a bewildered-looking* FATHER DROBNEY. *Crosses* D.L.C.) Mom, Dad. Hey, look who I met.

MAGEE. Father Drobney—what brings you down here!

DROBNEY. I heard so much commotion today and I met this young lady in the hall upstairs—

MAGEE. These are the Hollanders. They came here today in much the same way you did six years ago.

DROBNEY. Are you refugees?

WALTER. (*Rises.*) Refugees? You know what I paid for this shirt?

MARION. We were at the Vatican. We saw your boss. (*PHONE rings. She and* MAGEE *go for it,* MAGEE *gets it first.*) If it's for me I'm free to talk.

MAGEE. (*Into phone.*) Hello. Yes—I better take this inside. Excuse me a moment. (*Exits* R.)

SUSAN. He's got a little tiny room on the top floor and he practically never leaves it.

WALTER. (*Crosses to* DROBNEY.) Don't you go crazy?

DROBNEY. I am a guest through the courtesy of your government and I do not wish to make myself a nuisance.

MARION. Can't you ever leave here?

DROBNEY. Only if there is some drastic change in national policy. I have many friends who could help me to escape. But my duty is to return and some day lead my people once again.

MARION. But until you lead your people—you stay in your bedroom?

DROBNEY. In recent years I have developed a hobby and so it passes the lonely moments.

MARION. What do you do?

SUSAN. Father Drobney is a magician.

DROBNEY. I've been practicing for years. Years.

MARION. That's a wonderful hobby.

DROBNEY. (*Pulling cards from pocket and offering pack to* WALTER.) Pick a card—go ahead—any card . . . I'm not forcing!

WALTER. (*Sits* L.C. *chair.*) It's all I needed!

SUSAN. (*Crosses to* U.S. *of* L.C. *chair.*) C'mon, Dad. Be a sport.

DROBNEY. Go on—take any card . . .

MARION. Walter. Don't be rude.

(WALTER *reluctantly does.*)

DROBNEY. Jack of spades.

WALTER. Wrong, five of diamonds.

DROBNEY. Damn it! Sorry. (*Crosses himself, looking upward.*)

SUSAN. Father Drobney has all kinds of interesting things up there. Don't you, Father?

DROBNEY. Doves—I have white doves—I raised them! I transform them before your eyes!

SUSAN. Why don't you get some of your things—I'd love to see them!

DROBNEY. (*Becoming excited.*) Really? Would you?

MARION. Of course he would, wouldn't you, Walter?

WALTER. Of course, why do you think I had us trapped here.

DROBNEY. (*A step* U.S.) I'll be down in a minute. An audience! An audience! I'll do the rings and my silk handkerchief production and my vanishing billiard balls.

WALTER. Terrific. It's the Ed Sullivan Show.

DROBNEY. (*Crosses* U.L.) I'll be right down. (*Starts to exit, then as an afterthought returns and says to them all:*) Don't go away. (*Exits upstairs.*)

WALTER. (*Sarcastically.*) Don't go away.

SUSAN. Imagine staying in your room and practicing magic for six years.

MARION. (*Crosses* C.) What about us, Walter, what if the same thing happens to us?

WALTER. (*Rises and crosses to* MARION.) Where do you compare? We're innocent tourists. He's a priest. I'm sure he could get out of here if he made some effort, but you know how it is with those guys. The one who suffers the most gets a promotion.

KILROY. (*Enters* U.L. *and crosses* D.L.C.) Mr. Hollander, I think we've solved your dinner problem.

WALTER. What?

KILROY. The chef is making you hare.

WALTER. What?

KILROY. Hare.

WALTER. What's hare?

SUSAN. Rabbit.

WALTER. Pardon me?

MARION. Hare is rabbit.

KILROY. It's the closest thing to chicken the chef could find.

WALTER. Rabbit?

KILROY. It's delicious.

WALTER. Bunny rabbit?

MARION. If you don't ask him, he eats what you put in front of him.

WALTER. You mean a rabbit? Like Peter Rabbit?

KILROY. If I told you it was chicken you wouldn't know the difference.

WALTER. (*Exploding.*) I will not eat my furry friends! It's like eating squirrels . . . Look, can't you order out? There must be a Chinese Restaurant in town.

(KILROY *exits* U.L.)

DROBNEY. (*Re-enters* U.L. *overloaded with all kinds of colorful magical apparatus.*) I'm back.

WALTER. (*Crosses to desk.* MARION *crosses to* D.R.) He's back.

DROBNEY. (*Crosses to desk, puts gear down.*) I could only carry the small things, but it's enough for the first few hours of the show.

MARION. Er—how many hours does the show last?

DROBNEY. Hold this. (*Hands her a cane which turns into flowers upon her grasping it.*)

WALTER. (*Takes flowers. Moaning to himself.*) I want to go home.

DROBNEY. (*Light bulb flashing in his hand, hands it to* SUSAN.) I have dreamed of this moment for years. What miracle shall I start with?

MARION. I don't know—can you walk on water?

WALTER. (*Sits sofa. Moaning.*) My son is twelve years old. I won't see him again till he's eighteen.

DROBNEY. As you can observe—I have nothing up my robes.

MARION. (*Sits* L.C. *chair.*) Isn't it wonderful, Walter— a tricky priest.

DROBNEY. (*Pattering as he displays apparatus.*) I have nothing up my cylinder. I have nothing in my cage. Watch closely. I take this white dove and place it in here. Say the magic words . . . I remove this cylinder and where there was previously a dove—*voilà.* (*He looks and*

is surprised to find an empty cage. Looks under desk.)
Where's the rabbit? I had a rabbit in there. (*Crosses to*
MARION. *Getting frantic.*) Where's my rabbit?

(WALTER *rises.*)

CHEF. (*Enters* U.L., *holding live rabbit and goes to*
WALTER.) How do you like it? Rare, medium, well done?
DROBNEY. There's my rabbit!

(DROBNEY *goes for* CHEF, CHEF *runs,* WALTER *is run-*
ning from CHEF, MARION *is ducking to avoid getting*
trampled. The room is bedlam.)

MAGEE. (*Enters* R.) Now just a minute. This is a
United States Embassy and I mean to run it like one!

(*By now it is a madhouse and we:*)

BLACKOUT

ACT ONE

SCENE 3

LIGHTS up on MAGEE *on phone. It is five days later*
and looks it. MARION *irons in her robe, holding her*
bag on her arm. The room is messier and items of
clothes, either drying or just strewn about on chairs,
etc.

MAGEE. (*On phone.*) Mr. Krojack, your charges of espionage are ridiculous! They're tourists and we will not turn
them over to you . . . No, you will not wait them out.
They've been here five days and they're prepared to stay
five years if necessary. . . . (MARION *crosses and puts*
ironed shirt on desk, then crosses back.) Don't threaten

me. And don't threaten them. . . . (*Picks up shirt and waves it.*) You know you're only doing this because we captured Adolph Lopert, your illustrious Grey Fox. . . . I— Hello— Hello. (*Hangs up in disgust.*)

MARION. (*Ironing.*) Boy, they're stinkers.

MAGEE. Mrs. Hollander. Could you please remove this ironing board?

MARION. Where should I iron? If I go in the kitchen the chef starts to cry.

MAGEE. (*Exasperated.*) If everyone would please go to their room.

MARION. (*Crosses toward him.*) How much can a person keep locked up in a cloak room? Listen, I'm worried about Walter. First he wrote his Congressman and he got back a mimeographed form letter. Then he wrote his Senator and he got back a mimeographed form letter, then he wrote our son and he got back a mimeographed form letter. "I am okay. I am eating. I am getting plenty of rest. I will consider any suggestions you make. Your loving son, Seth."

MAGEE. That's because he writes him three letters a day. He worries about that boy too much. There's no need for your husband to send him food from Europe. Please remove that ironing board.

(*She begins to fold ironing board.* WALTER *enters and crosses in his robe and underwear.*)

MARION. Hello, Walter. (WALTER *ignores it and exits.*) You see that. I said, Hello Walter. You see the look he gave me? (*Following him off* U.L., *carrying ironing board.*) Hello, Grouch.

MAGEE. (*Goes after her when* KILROY *enters* R.) Mrs. Hol—

KILROY. (*Crosses to desk.*) He should be here any minute.

MAGEE. (*Crosses toward him.*) Who should?

KILROY. The Sultan of Bashir. Or did you forget?

MAGEE. The Sultan? Wasn't that called off?

KILROY. I suggested a postponement but you assured everyone you would have matters settled and that business would proceed as usual.

MAGEE. Oh, hell. Let me think.

KILROY. You know the Sultan is a dictator and a very temperamental man. Any little ripple could hurt your father's oil deal and I'd hate to be in your shoes if that happens. (*Exits* R.)

MAGEE. Maybe I can still call him and delay it. (*Exits* R.)

WALTER. (*Entering with* MARION U.L.) I got a telegram this morning. Sam Blackwell caters a sweet-sixteen party.

MARION. (*Carrying a basket. Crosses to sofa.*) I don't want to hear.

WALTER. (*Follows her.*) He gets a special price on the meats—

MARION. (*Sits sofa, takes socks from basket.*) I'm not interested.

WALTER. He doesn't use our regular guy, ya hear? Tries to buy cheap.

MARION. I'm not listening.

WALTER. Four guests go home that night and what happens? They get food poisoning.

MARION. (*Rising.*) Ohmigod—

WALTER. They're in the hospital. Because he looked for bargains.

MARION. I'll bet they're suing.

WALTER. Aha! Now you wanna hear!

MARION. Are they?

WALTER. (*Crosses* C.) I don't want to tell you—you're not interested.

MARION. Tell me!

WALTER. No, listen, you're not interested, why should I tell you—?

MARION. Tell me.

WALTER. (*Crosses* L.C. *Hands over ears, he sings.*)

Hmmm, hmmm, hmmm . . . "A foggy day in London town . . . It had me low—"

MARION. Walter. You know what you are? You are a sadist.

WALTER. Why? A minute ago you weren't interested.

MARION. I'm not interested.

WALTER. You're not? Good. "A foggy day . . ."

MARION. Grouch. Are you gonna answer me?

WALTER. (*Crosses toward her.*) Are they suing? Is that what you asked? No, they're not suing. They're not suing. We're suing them for low resistance to tainted meat.

MARION. Walter—

WALTER. Of course they're suing. What do you expect from poisoned people?

MARION. Ohmigod!

WALTER. If I could get Sam Blackwell here, I'd crush his head!

MARION. Be thankful nobody died.

WALTER. Yes, Marion—we're thinking of making that our slogan.

DROBNEY. (*Enters from upstairs, struggling to get out of a straitjacket. Crosses D.L.C.*) Excuse me. Will someone help me out of this?

WALTER. Not now with the magic tricks.

DROBNEY. I don't know how Houdini used to get out of this.

MARION. (*Putting basket on desk and going to DROBNEY's aid.*) Don't pay any attention to him, Father. I think it's marvelous a man of the cloth has a hobby besides just God.

WALTER. (*Crosses toward DROBNEY.*) A person builds a catering firm for twenty years, he goes away and leaves his partner in charge. He begins poisoning customers. I'm working with Lucrezia Borgia!

DROBNEY. Faith in the Lord, my son.

WALTER. I have faith in the Lord, Father; if he can hear me now—please crush Sam Blackwell's head.

(PHONE rings. MARION gets it.)

MARION. Hello? . . . What? . . . Yes? . . . No, hold it . . . It's New Jersey for you. Must be Sam Blackwell. Be nice. We all make mistakes.

(She hands WALTER the phone as she proceeds to help DROBNEY struggle out of his straitjacket. Throughout the following she and DROBNEY get entangled and drop to floor.)

WALTER. Hello? . . . yes . . . yes, this is he . . . yes . . . go ahead . . . Hello, cretin. How are you, cretin? Poison any more people, cretin? How many? . . . Wonderful. Keep up the good work . . . Two more keeled over—they're dropping like flies. Murderer? . . . Murderer . . . I can't hear you. Talk louder, murderer. . . . Well, what did the lawyer say? . . . Oh, really? He feels they have a case, eh? . . . Blackwell, when I get back to the States, I'm going to rent a car and run you over—you understand? . . . Hello? . . . Murderer, I can't hear you, Blackwell. . . . Louder. . . . Overseas Operator, I can't hear the murderer . . . Blackwell—you're finished as a caterer—you've mixed your last fruit compote.

(By now MARION and DROBNEY are a tangled blob on the floor. Her hairpiece has come off. WALTER is on phone yelling and with room in chaos, who enters but the SULTAN of Bashir and his veiled WIFE. He is a huge imposing desert chieftain in full robes with dark glasses and beard. BURNS precedes him in by a few steps U.R.)

BURNS. Mr. Magee—His Majesty has arrived— Ohmigod! Mr. Magee! Mr. Magee! *(Seeing the situation, he runs off R. to get MAGEE.)*

(SULTAN stares face to face with WALTER who has just

hung up phone. The SULTAN *also sees* MARION *and* DROBNEY *on the floor, the priest still in his straightjacket. He drinks it in. Finally.*)

WALTER. (*Crosses to* SULTAN.) What have we got here? Lawrence of Arabia.

MARION. (*Extricating herself, curtsying.*) How do you do, Sultan?

WALTER. Sultan? You know him?

MARION. Are you ignorant? It's the Sultan of Bashir.

WALTER. What do you do? Hang around the U.N. building, picking up Arabs?

SULTAN. I am His Royal Majesty, Ruler of the People of Bashir. I am here to see Ambassador Magee.

MARION. How do you do?

SULTAN. This is my wife.

MARION. (*To* WIFE.) Hello. Can I take your veil?

WALTER. I'm Walter Hollander from New Jersey. (DROBNEY *tries wrenching free from jacket but fails.*) Drobney, you'll have a heart attack—you're not a young man.

DROBNEY. (*Embarrassed, he thrashes out of the room and up the stairs.*) Excuse me, Your Majesty.

SULTAN. I am a guest of Ambassador Magee's.

MARION. (*Trying to be polite.*) I hope you didn't have any trouble getting by all those soldiers around the Embassy. Walter and I are wanted.

WALTER. (*Dawning on him.*) I know where I read about the Sultan of Bashir recently—didn't you fellas put down an uprising?

SULTAN. Eh?

WALTER. Didn't you have some kind of revolution or something?

SULTAN. Where's the Ambassador?

WALTER. (*Not really unfriendly.*) Sure . . . you killed all those workers . . . I read about it. That wasn't nice what you did to those people—they were protesting peacefully.

SULTAN. There are two sides to that affair, my friend.

WALTER. (*Still innocently enough.*) What kind of two sides? A few poor workers go on strike—you gotta shoot 'em?

SULTAN. If you could see them. They are vermin. There's no other way to teach them.

(WALTER *regards this with growing irritation.*)

MARION. Er, Walter—what are you talking about something you know nothing about?

WALTER. (*Getting a bit annoyed.*) I don't know politics? What's the matter with you? Don't you read the papers? This guy executes his people like you use your Charge-A-Plate.

MARION. You're in a bad mood.

SULTAN. I did not come here to be received by a pair of dogs. Where is the Ambassador?

WALTER. (*Dealing this square into the* SULTAN's *face.*) I always read things in the papers and I get frustrated because being a little shot from New Jersey I never get a chance to express my opinion to a real big shot.

MARION. No one asked you.

MAGEE. (*Enters* R. *just in time to prevent what might have turned into a pushing match.*) Your Majesty— forgive us.

SULTAN. I will not stay here unless I receive an apology from your government.

MAGEE. Mr. Hollander—leave this room at once.

WALTER. (*To* SULTAN.) What's your trouble, Aladdin?

MARION. Walter, you're in a very bad mood this morning. Let's go.

WALTER. I live here. I'm not going any place. I pay taxes. Why, 'cause this bum has some oil wells?

MAGEE. Your Majesty, please come inside.

SULTAN. You are an insolent swine!

WALTER. I'll hit him a shot in the chops, they'll have to bandage him in his own sheets!

SULTAN. Don't threaten me, you pig.

WALTER. (*To* MAGEE.) What is this guy doing here anyway?

MAGEE. That's none of your business.

WALTER. This is my business. I pay taxes. This building is rented with my money.

MARION. Walter, butt out.

WALTER. I don't like the idea of my government doing business with this guy.

MAGEE. Mr. Hollander, that's something for the government to decide.

WALTER. I am the government!

MARION. Listen to him. He's the government.

WALTER. What do you think the government is? It's little people like you and me! (*Then considers her in her robe.*) Well, maybe not you.

SULTAN. I have never been insulted in such a manner.

MAGEE. Your Majesty, I beg your forgiveness.

WALTER. Take a walk, fatso! That's how this country gets into trouble. Dealing with guys like him!

MARION. In your opinion.

WALTER. Yeah. Read Walter Lippmann!

SULTAN. I did not come here to be humiliated. Relations between us are at an end. (*He and his* WIFE *move to exit* U.R. *in a huff.*)

MAGEE. (*Follows placatingly.*) Your Majesty! . . .

(*They go off,* MAGEE *in pursuit.*)

WALTER. (*Crosses* U.R.) And every time you bring somebody into this house who's a bum like him—they get the same. Come on, Marion. (*Walks off in opposite direction,* L., *proudly.*)

MARION. (*Getting her basket and following* WALTER *off, she takes a parting shot at him.*) For a man who cheats on his income tax, you're certainly a big shot.

BLACKOUT

ACT ONE

SCENE 4

As lights go on, MAGEE is on phone. It is later that night. As usual, MAGEE is having a hard time of it.

MAGEE. Dad. . . . Dad. . . . (*Rises and takes a step* L.) It wasn't my fault. Mr. Hollander insulted him. . . . But, Dad, you said it would look bad for the family image if you put Mr. Kilroy in charge— (KILROY *enters.*) Dad?. . . Yes, Dad. . . . Yes, sir. . . . Goodbye. (*Hangs up.*)

KILROY. I'll start right away to see if I can arrange a spy trade. Hard luck, Magee, but those are the breaks. (*Exits* R.)

SUSAN. (*Enters* U.L. *with drink.*) Hi, Axel. I brought you a drink. (*Crossing to him.*) I thought you might need one.

MAGEE. Why? Why does it always happen? What do I do? I'll kill myself—that's it—I'm gonna kill myself—

SUSAN. Axel, what happened?

MAGEE. (*Crosses to* L.C. *chair and sits.*) I'm a failure— I'm thirty years old and a failure—not just a *little* failure—I'm a *big* failure—like the World's Fair.

SUSAN. Have a drink.

MAGEE. (*Rises and crosses around* L. *chair.*) I've been relieved of my command by Kilroy and the United States Weather Bureau has declared me a disaster area.

SUSAN. Your job really means a lot to you, doesn't it?

MAGEE. (*Crosses* R.C.) I guess it's hard to understand. It's all I've been brought up to think of.

SUSAN. I understand. It's not easy to be the son of a famous person.

MAGEE. Susan— Do you know that when I was ten years old and I did something wrong, my mother used to hit me with a copy of Time Magazine with my father's picture on the cover. (*Sits on sofa arm.*)

SUSAN. (*Crosses to him.*) Oh, Axel. I don't find you a failure. Maybe you're just in the wrong field. Maybe in some other business you'd be a genius.

MAGEE. Sure, if there was such a thing as the failure business—I'd have chain stores. What does your fiancé do?

SUSAN. He's a lawyer.

MAGEE. I know it's none of my business, but you don't seem wildly enthused over the prospect of getting married.

SUSAN. I'm not getting married. I haven't told my parents yet but I have told Donald. Donald's bright and *very* handsome but—not for me.

MAGEE. (*Rises, suddenly heartened.*) I see. Ahem. I guess your father will be disappointed.

SUSAN. Oh, he's going to have a stroke. He adores Donald.—And compared to the kind of boys I almost married; Donald's the answer to a father's prayer.

MAGEE. Have you almost married often?

SUSAN. A few times—and always the type that would turn my father's hair grey. A manic-depressive jazz musician—a draft dodger, and a defrocked priest.

MAGEE. Boy, you must really hate the suburbs.

SUSAN. If I tie myself down for life I want someone—

MAGEE. Stable and successful—

SUSAN. No. I want a little action.

MAGEE. (*Quick to agree.*) That's what I mean. You don't want anything too stable or successful.

SUSAN. The truth is you never know what you want. You think you want a certain type and then you meet somebody who has nothing of what you want and for some unexplainable reason you fall in love with him.

MAGEE. I know. I once wrote a poem about that.

SUSAN. A poem? Axel, you're a latent creator. Is the place still heavily surrounded?

MAGEE. Yes. You wanna see? (*Crosses to switch and turns out LIGHT. Suddenly the mood is romantic.*)

SUSAN. (*Peering out window.*) Look at all those stars. You can see the dipper, see?

(*As she looks,* MAGEE *is sneaking up behind her meaning to grab her and kiss her. She turns abruptly and he rapidly tries to fake being casual by leaning against office door relaxedly. Unfortunately, the office door is wide open and his attempt to lean on it sends him hurtling out of the room. He re-enters trying to make small of his weird-looking clumsiness.*)

MAGEE. Sorry. Um, the air is so clear this time of year.

SUSAN. (*Turning to window.*) I love fall. It's such an exciting time of year. It's the start of everything.

MAGEE. (*Beginning to creep up behind her for another try.*) I like winter. Because I love to ski.

SUSAN. I've never gone skiing but I'm mad for the idea.

MAGEE. Maybe someday when all this gets worked out I could take you skiing. I know you'd love it. It's very romantic. I broke my pelvis once. (*Realizing what he said he buries his face in his hands as if to say, "Why do I always screw up?"*)

SUSAN. (*Turns.*) Well, it's very late.—I better go to bed. Good night, Axel. It was fun talking to you.

MAGEE. Thanks for the—drink—

(*Suddenly grabs her, tries to kiss her, they* BOTH *topple over the sofa and she splatters on the floor.*)

SUSAN. Whaaa—?

MAGEE. (*Around* R. *of sofa.*) I'm sorry! Are you okay?

SUSAN. (*Getting up and backing off from this maniac toward desk.*) I better go now.

MAGEE. (*Trying to go to her and help her.*) Please forgive me—I—I—

SUSAN. (*Running for her life to stairs.*) Excuse me.

MAGEE. (*Follows to stairs.*) I'm awfully sorry. Are you all right?

SUSAN. I'm okay. Good night. (*She bolts up the stairs.*)

MAGEE. (*Calling up to her.*) Good night. I'm sorry
. . . I—DAMMIT! (*Crosses to desk.*) Why can't I do
anything right! (*He kicks table out of anger and suc-
ceeds only in hurting his toe.*) Eoowwwww! (*As he dances
wildly on one foot, in pain, we:*)

BLACKOUT

ACT ONE

SCENE 5

Lights up on WALTER. *It is several days later. He is on
    phone and radiates excitement. He is dressed as
    when he first came on, in same shirt, hat.*

WALTER. Son, we'll be home tonight. . . . That's right,
boy, we're being traded for a Communist spy. A big
spy. . . . Oh, it's a terrific thing. You'll read about it
in the papers. (MARION *enters* L. *dressed for travel,
lugging all the family suitcases, which she puts down* L.
of desk.) Is there anything you want us to bring you?
. . . Anything from here? (*To* MARION.) He wants us
to take some pictures! (*Back into phone.*) Cretin. . . .
We'll see you later and don't forget to thank Mrs.
Klein. (*Hangs up.*) I called Donald last night.
    MARION. *You* called Donald? Don't you think that's
Susan's business?
    WALTER. Ah, I feel she neglects him. Besides, I want
to establish good relations with my future son-in-law.
    MARION. What'd he say?
    WALTER. He wasn't home. My future attorney was in
court—suing a slum landlord. The boy is a poet.
    MARION. I called Barney Silverman—he rented the
station wagon again.
    WALTER. (*Crosses* L.C.) Good, on the way home he
can drop me at work.

MARION. (*Crosses toward him.*) You're not coming home first?

WALTER. What for?

MARION. You're going directly from Europe to work?

WALTER. Why not?

MARION. Are you crazy?

WALTER. (*A step* L.) I'll help with the unpacking when I come home at seven.

MARION. You haven't seen our apartment in six weeks—

WALTER. Who was there to change it?

MARION. A man hasn't seen his apartment in six weeks —he's going to work first?

WALTER. It's a Thursday—I always work Thursday.

MARION. The business can't wait another day?

WALTER. (*Exiting* L.) What do you care?

MARION. (*Following him off* L.) If I cash in our Mutual Funds, will you see a psychiatrist?

(SUSAN *enters* U.L. *with suitcase.* MAGEE *enters* R. *taking suitcase to aid* SUSAN.)

MAGEE. All packed?

SUSAN. It was clever of Mr. Kilroy to arrange this spy exchange, Axel.

MAGEE. (*Puts suitcase down near desk.*) Yes, he's very efficient. He's already lined up a big reception for the Sultan of Bashir this weekend and I'm sure he'll smooth that situation over as quickly as he did this. I guess some just have the knack.

SUSAN. I'd still rather be you.

MAGEE. I'm going to miss you, Susan.

SUSAN. If you're ever in Newark—

MAGEE. At the rate I'm going it could happen. (*Crosses to sofa.*)

SUSAN. Axel—I'm sorry about the other night.

MAGEE. *You're* sorry?

SUSAN. (*Crosses toward him.*) I'm sorry I got so

shaken up. It was something I wanted you to do and when you did it I got shaken up.

MAGEE. I wish we could have spent some time together.

SUSAN. So do I. Well—at least you'll still have your job.

MAGEE. Yeah.

MARION. (*Entering after* WALTER L., BOTH *with more luggage.* BOTH *cross* D.L.) I can't understand you— they've been so nice to us here, how can you stick their towels in your suitcase?

WALTER. It's habit . . . I was a deprived child. (*They put suitcases down* D.S. *of desk.*)

MARION. You sure it's safe to go out there?

MAGEE. It's all been carefully worked out. Mr. Krojack will accompany you to the plane.

MARION. (*Crosses to* SUSAN.) Did you take your hair dryer out of Mr. Burns' office?

DROBNEY. (*Enters with* CHEF U.L.) We came to say goodbye and to wish you good luck.

CHEF. (*You can tell he doesn't mean it.*) Yes— It's a pity you're leaving.

WALTER. (*Joshing him.*) If you ever need a job, Chef, I could probably get you one at Chock Full O'Nuts.

CHEF. I may as well tell you, Mr. Hollander, the veal you had last night was eel. And you cleaned your plate.

WALTER. Look in the vase next to the dining room table.

(*Outraged, the* CHEF *exits* U.L.)

DROBNEY. Bless you all . . . you have made my life richer. (DROBNEY *appears to want to shake hands but offers deck of cards instead.* WALTER *picks one good-naturedly.*) Five of diamonds.

WALTER. (*Amazed.*) Right. (*Then he grabs deck from* DROBNEY *to examine them.*) They're all five of diamonds.

(DROBNEY *exits* U.L.)

KILROY. (*Enters* U.R.) Mr. Krojack has arrived.

KROJACK. (*Enters* U.R.) So, we finally meet face to face.

WALTER. We don't hold a grudge.

MARION. Sure—you can't with the H-bomb.

WALTER. Let bygones be bygones.

KROJACK. (*Booming.*) Criminals against the State!

MARION. Take it easy, mister, you'll live longer.

KROJACK. Only for Adolph Lopert, The Grey Fox, would our government do this.

KILROY. Mr. Magee, will you check and see that the Hollanders haven't left anything?

MAGEE. I think there's a couple of cartons upstairs. (*He and* SUSAN *go upstairs.*)

MARION. (*Last minute rummage through her purse.*) I better make sure Walter took his passport. Wouldn't it be a scream if you had to spend the rest of your life on Ellis Island? (*Exits upstairs.*)

BURNS. (*Enters* R.) Mr. Kilroy—there's a phone call for you and it's urgent. It's Ambassador Magee's private line.

(*Exits with* KILROY, R., *leaving* KROJACK *and* WALTER *alone, face to face. The air is ridden with tension.* WALTER *finally waves his finger at* KROJACK *as if to say "Hi."*)

KROJACK. (*With ugliness.*) If I could have my way— you and all those like you would hang in the public square as an example to all enemies of the State.

WALTER. Krojack, when was the last time you called up a girl and she said "Yes?"

KROJACK. I have men who worked with the Gestapo during the war. One hour at their disposal and you would tell everything.

WALTER. Tell what? Who's got what to tell?

KROJACK. Admit it! You are a filthy American spy!

WALTER. Who? What?

KROJACK. (*Pressing him.*) Admit it!

WALTER. Who?

KROJACK. (*On top of him.*) Admit it!

WALTER. What?

KROJACK. (*Screaming.*) Admit it!

WALTER. (*Enough already.*) Okay. I admit it! If it makes you happy. I admit it. I'm not a caterer. I'm not from New Jersey. She's not my wife, she's a U-Boat Commander. You happy?—You're supposed to be so clever—you're nothing! (*Crosses* D.S. *of table.*) This was my easiest caper since the Kowalski wedding.

KROJACK. (*Uncontrollably enraged, he starts for* WALTER.) I will kill you myself!

WALTER. (*Turns brandishing hand to chop.*) I wouldn't try anything if I were you. We're all trained in karate, you know— Ah— (*Jumps.*) Ah— (*Jumps, assuming another position.*) Ahh— (*Chops hand down on coffee table to demonstrate his strength and surprises himself and* KROJACK *by cracking table in two.*)

KROJACK. If my hands were not tied by stupid red tape, I would have my men come in here and drag you out.

WALTER. It riles you, doesn't it? You like to bully people, don't you? Wait'll I get back home and tell the newspapers how we made monkeys out of you. You'll be the laughing stock of the Secret Police. I wouldn't be surprised if they take away your disguise kit.

KROJACK. (*Taunted, he goes for* WALTER *again.*) You will die. I will see to it. If I must do it with my bare hands.

WALTER. (*Thrusting hand in his jacket pocket and faking that he has a gun.*) Don't make a move or I'll blow you to pieces.

KROJACK. You're bluffing.

WALTER. Oh, yeah, big shot? (*Pulls out hand which he holds in shape of gun and sticks it up against* KROJACK'S *face, having been carried away.*)

KROJACK. Ha ha. You fool. That's a finger!

WALTER. It may look like a finger—but it's a flesh-colored .45 with two joints, a knuckle and a little hair. (*Puts it back in pocket.*)

KROJACK. Idiot.

MARION. (*Enters U.L., followed by* SUSAN *and* MAGEE *carrying final luggage, and crossing with it D.R. of desk.*) Walter, I'm ready to go. (*She and* SUSAN *cross U.L.C*)

WALTER. (*Sweating, but one up on* KROJACK.) Me too. You got everything?

KROJACK. I had finally convinced the authorities to let me use my own methods of dealing with you. This trade has cheated me out of that and has saved your lives. But someday we will meet again. (*He and* WALTER *face to face, adversaries.*)

KILROY. (*Enters R., white-faced, crosses to L. of sofa.*) The deal is off.

MAGEE. What?

KILROY. I have just received word from our Intelligence. Adolph Lopert is dead.

KROJACK. (*Stunned.*) Dead?

KILROY. He has hung himself in his cell.

KROJACK. (*Can't believe it.*) Dead? Adolph Lopert is dead?

WALTER. (*Also stunned, crossing to* KILROY.) He's dead? He's not alive? He's dead? (*With a look at the vicious* KROJACK.) Oh boy, am I in trouble. (*Crossing to* MARION.)

KROJACK. The Grey Fox dies by his own hand. I must go back to my office immediately. (*To* WALTER.) So we *shall* meet again . . . and soon. (*Exits U.R. as does* KIL-ROY, *who goes to show him out.*)

MARION. Walter. What are we going to do?

WALTER. (*Shaky.*) We're not going home?

MAGEE. I—guess not . . .

WALTER. (*Musing, glassy-eyed.*) He had to pick today to hang himself. He couldn't wait till the week end? It's a holiday week end.

MARION. See, and you wanted to rush to work. I better call Barney Silverman.

WALTER. (*Crosses to* L.C *chair.*) I'm getting drowsy.

MARION. Drowsy?

WALTER. (*Sits.*) I already took a dramamine. (*They ALL look at him.*) It's a half hour before take-off! They caught him seven days ago, he had all this time, he had to pick today. And this morning yet.

MARION. (*Crosses to* L. *of desk.*) It's five a.m. there —he did it before breakfast. See how important it is to eat. Well, we better unpack. (*Goes to get bags.*)

WALTER. (*Rises.*) I'll call Seth and tell him to go ahead with his application to the Foster Parents' home. (*And he goes off* L.)

SUSAN. (*Musing.*) What makes a man kill himself?

MARION. What do you expect from a Grey Fox. Is that a name for a grown-up person? (*Goes off* L. *dejectedly with luggage.*)

SUSAN. (*Alone with* MAGEE.) Well, you wanted us to spend more time together.

(*They stare at one another with mixed feelings, then he takes her and kisses her. She responds. In the midst, WALTER re-enters* L.)

WALTER. Magee, do you think it's possible—? Uhh— oh boy—oh boy—Marion, come quickly—she's *kissing* the failure!

BLACKOUT

ACT TWO

Scene 1

Stage is empty and DROBNEY *once again comes downstairs and addresses audience.*

DROBNEY. (*Crosses* D.L.C.) While you were out smoking, the Hollanders have been living here nearly two weeks now and everyone is really feeling the strain. Mrs. Hollander has nothing to do and so she goes around all day cleaning the Embassy.

(*Enter* MARION U.R. *with feather duster. She dusts about and says:*)

MARION. I've waxed every floor in the house today twice. Even the rooms with wall-to-wall carpeting. (*Exits* U.R.)

DROBNEY. (*Crosses* D.R.C.) It's nice to be clean but a lot of floor wax is a dangerous thing.

KILROY. (*Crosses rapidly, his arm in a sling,* U.L. *to* L.) Goddamn living room floor. (*Exits* L.)

DROBNEY. (*Crosses* D.R.) Susan and Magee feel a different kind of strain.

SUSAN. (*Enters in love, with* MAGEE U.L. *They cross to* D.C.) I wish there was someplace we could go to be alone.

MAGEE. Your father watches us like a hawk. Last night when he thought we were going to meet in the dining room he squatted motionless, put a throw-pillow on his lap and pretended to be a chair.

SUSAN. You're kidding!

MAGEE. No! I sat on him!

49

(*They exit* R.)

DROBNEY. .(*Crosses* D.L.) If Mr. Hollander's behavior seems a little extreme, it's only because he is a man torn between a failing business, a failing future son-in-law, and a twelve-year-old boy that he misses very much.

(*Enter* WALTER, L., *composing letter.*)

WALTER. Dear Seth, don't forget to dress warmly. And eat slowly. Chew your food carefully, and go to bed early, and stay away from women. See what happened to me? (*And he's off* R.)

DROBNEY. After thinking it over very carefully and weighing the pros and cons, I had a long talk with Mrs. Hollander and Susan, about the only way to see their home again. ESCAPE!

(MARION *and* SUSAN *steal on from opposite upstage entrances and cross* D.C.)

MARION. Did Father Drobney speak to you about an escape?

SUSAN. Yes. I think it's a wonderful idea!

MARION. Did you suggest it to Mr. Magee?

SUSAN. Not yet. I want to wait till the moment's right. Did you suggest it to Daddy?

MARION. I wouldn't dare. You know how he hates to take me anyplace. (*They exit separately,* U.L. *and* U.R.)

(MAGEE *enters,* R., *looks out window.*)

DROBNEY. (*Crosses to him.*) Hello, Magee.

MAGEE. (*Turns in.*) Hello, Father. I didn't want to alarm anybody but I don't like what's happening out there. This morning there were just a few pickets in front of the building. The number's been growing and now there's dozens. And a lot of them look too old to be students to me.

DROBNEY. (*Crosses to desk.*) Ah, yes, I see. Some are not students. Some are Communist agitators.

MAGEE. (*Crosses to him.*) Well, just how ominous are those anti-Hollander signs they're carrying?

DROBNEY. Is there a safe place to hide the Hollanders in the event of serious rioting?

MAGEE. Serious rioting? What do you have in mind?

DROBNEY. Stoning, looting, fires.

MAGEE. Stoning, looting, fires. My life is like the Old Testament. The only thing I've been able to avoid so far is locusts.

DROBNEY. The Hollanders are enemies of the State. Krojack has many followers who will stop at nothing. If they choose to they will find a way to come in here and get the Hollanders out. (*Starts to exit L.*)

MAGEE. (*Following.*) See, Kilroy doesn't understand the danger of these things. He lacks my vast experience getting stoned and spit at. I better call my father direct and let him know there may be trouble.

(DROBNEY *exits* L. WALTER *and* MARION *enter* U.L. *just as* MAGEE *is about to exit after* DROBNEY.)

WALTER. I want to speak to you.

MAGEE. Later, Mr. Hollander. (*And he exits* L.)

WALTER. (*Crosses* D.L.C.) All of a sudden it's goodbye successful lawyer, hello psychotic diplomat!

MARION. (*Follows.*) It's her own life, Walter. She's twenty-three.

WALTER. Who says it's not her own life. I just want her to do the right thing, that's all. . . .

MARION. So.

WALTER. So, what I tell her is the right thing. This guy is what we used to call in the pool room, a loser!

MARION. He's a Yale graduate.

WALTER. Yale makes mistakes too. (*Crosses to sofa.*)

MARION. Walter, don't get involved.

WALTER. This is the worst prospect she's ever had. I

like even the draft dodger she was going with better because he at least was a success—he beat the draft—something! (*Sits.*)

MARION. (*Crosses* C.) May I remind you that when I
married you, your future didn't look too secure.

WALTER. That's different—where do you compare—I
have a *joie de vivre*—

MARION. What good is security if she's not happy?

WALTER. (*Rises and crosses to her.*) Where does happy
come into this? I'm talking about marriage! When you
get married you give up happiness! All of a sudden
Donald can't make her happy? He's an attorney—he has
court cases, he'll fill out briefs, there's mortgages, there's
litigation—it's romantic. (*He removes some letters from
jacket and goes to stove.*)

MARION. She was always a little lukewarm about
Donald, I felt . . . . I didn't want to say anything—
Hey, what are you doing with the stove?

WALTER. This is a stove?

MARION. It's a porcelain-tiled stove. You think Europe
has central heating?

WALTER. I've been mailing letters in it. (*Puts letters
back in pocket dejectedly.*)

MARION. (*Crosses to* D.S. *of sofa. Hearing increased
NOISE from window.*) What is that? That must be those
pickets outside?

WALTER. (*Crosses to sofa.*) Marion, be careful. I
thought there was only a few . . .

MARION. (*Crosses and looks out window.*) Walter—
look what's doing out there—it's a regular demonstration.
Ohmigod! They have a cloth dummy that looks like you
and they're burning it.

(*Noise BUILDING.*)

WALTER. Maybe they think I'm a football coach.

MARION. Walter, this is not a joking matter. They got
big black ugly signs with our names on them.

(*NOISE very big now.*)

WALTER. Sticks and stones will break my bones but names will never harm me.

MARION. Walter, they have sticks and stones!

(*RIOT proportions.*)

WALTER. Come away from the *window!*

(*Sound of THREE SHOTS from other part of the house.*)

MARION. What was that?

(SUSAN *runs in* U.R., *frantic, crosses* D.R.C.)

SUSAN. (*Yelling to be heard above noise.*) They're shooting and throwing rocks through the windows! Mr. Kilroy got hit in the head with a brick. He's lying on the hall floor muttering something about aviation.

WALTER. Don't panic. Everybody remain *calm!* (*Sound: TWO GUNSHOTS through window.*) Okay— now you can panic!

SUSAN. (*To* L. *of desk.*) Duck! It's a riot!

(*They* ALL *hide behind sofa, under desk, tables.*)

WALTER. (*From the floor.*) Magee! Magee! Magee! Come quickly! We have your usual riot!

MARION. (*Under desk.*) Walter, what are we going to do?

WALTER. Try not to get *shot.*

(*More SHOOTING.*)

MARION. Walter—maybe if you went outside and addressed them.

WALTER. I said—let's go to Atlantic Beach—we'll swim—we'll play pinochle—

(MAGEE *bursts in* L. *and crosses* D.R.C., *crouching to avoid being hit. Two more GUNSHOTS are heard and a ticking TIME BOMB comes through the window and lands on the floor.*)

MAGEE. Is everybody all right?
SUSAN. Yes, are you?
WALTER. (*Who has gone to bomb and picked it up.*) What's this?
MAGEE. (*Noticing it in* WALTER's *hands.*) Be careful! That's a time bomb!
WALTER. A bo—bo—bo—bo——

(WALTER *throws it to* MAGEE *who tosses it back to* WALTER *in panic.*)

MAGEE. Don't put it down! The slightest tap could blow this place sky high!
WALTER. Agah-gah—don't anybody come near me!

(*The noise of the CROWD subsides.*)

MARION. (*Crosses to window.*) They're running away.
MAGEE. Everybody out of the room. Quickly!
MARION. Walter, keep calm!
WALTER. I'm calm. Who's Walter?
MAGEE. I've had experience with these things. (*Trying to fix it.*) If I can just dismantle it before it goes off—
WALTER. (*Sweating.*) Dismantle. Dismantle.
SUSAN. Axel—be careful.
WALTER. My leg itches.
MARION. Where does it itch, Walter, I'll scratch it!
WALTER. Get out of the room—everybody!
MARION. What about you?
WALTER. Look out the window—you'll see me passing over the house any minute.

MARION. (*Crosses to* SUSAN.) Come on, Susan—there's no sense in all of us getting torn limb from limb!

WALTER. Thanks, Marion.

MAGEE. (*Breathing a huge sigh as he disconnects it.*) There, it's dead. I did it.

WALTER. (*Crosses and sits* L.C. *chair. Sighing.*) My heart—my heart sounds like a discotheque.

MARION. (*Crosses to* WALTER.) Who tells you to pick up strange objects?

WALTER. That's how I met you!

BURNS. (*Enters* U.R. *and crosses to* L. *of sofa.*) Has anyone been hurt?

MAGEE. (*Crosses to him.*) We're okay—what about everyone else?

BURNS. Mr. Kilroy got hit in the head with a brick. He must have a concussion. He thinks he's the Wright Brothers.

MAGEE. (*To* BURNS.) Wright Brothers. Lodge a complaint at the ministry and report this to Washington. Tell them I tried reaching my father but he's on a yacht somewhere in the damn Caribbean.

KILROY. (*Enters, delirious,* U.R.) Come quickly, Wilbur. I'm coming, Orville. I'm telling you, Wilbur, we can do it. Do what? Get those machines to fly. Orville, you're crazy. But so are you. Let's go down to Kitty Hawk Friday and put it in the air. We'll do it. Both of us. What if it doesn't work, Orville? Wilbur, we must try it and stop this arguing. Orville, you always were Mother's favorite. (*And he's off* D.L.)

MAGEE. Mr. Burns, take Mr. Kilroy to his room and get the doctor over here immediately. We may have to check him into a hospital.

WALTER. You better get him twin beds.

(BURNS *exits* U.L.)

MARION. We better give Mr. Burns a hand, Walter. We may be next. (*They exit* U.L.)

MAGEE. (*Crosses to desk.*) In the absence of my superiors I have no choice but to give myself a battle-field commission. Until further notice, I am in charge of this Embassy.

SUSAN. How exciting.

MAGEE. (*A step D.S.*) Now if I could think of what to do it would help.

SUSAN. (*Crosses toward him.*) I can.

MAGEE. What?

SUSAN. Axel—supposing my parents and I escape?

MAGEE. By escape, you mean what?

SUSAN. By escape I mean to leave here and show up in Newark.

MAGEE. (*Crosses below.*) Susan, you're nuts.

SUSAN. Axel, I've already spoken to Father Drobney about it and he says we can do it.

MAGEE. Father Drobney! The Holy Houdini? He can't get himself out of a strait-jacket. What does he know?

SUSAN. He knows how to get us out of the country and he says it's a cinch. Axel, there's no other way!

MAGEE. (*A step L.*) Susan, why don't you get some rest and if you still feel the same way next year . . .

SUSAN. (*Step in.*) Why not? Give me one good reason.

MAGEE. Death, that's one good reason. If you think your father's uncomfortable here, wait'll you see him in front of a firing squad.

SUSAN. My parents are willing. We've already discussed it.

MAGEE. (*Crosses below.*) Then your parents should be locked up and since they are locked up—we have nothing to talk about.

SUSAN. Axel, I'm serious.

MAGEE. (*Crosses to sofa. Hands over his ears.*) "A foggy day . . ."

SUSAN. You have no imagination.

MAGEE. (*Sits.*) I have a wonderful imagination. Ten minutes after you try and escape I can picture Krojack wearing your father's shirt.

SUSAN. (*Crosses to him.*) Axel, why can't we escape?

MAGEE. I just gave you a good reason. An escape requires timing and coordination and good physical condition. Your father gets out of breath if I ask him to pass the salt.

SUSAN. (*Sits. Selling him.*) Oh, Axel, for once in your life take the initiative. Don't let things happen to you. We'll do it together. That's what life is. A series of adventures you go through with someone you care about. We can do it, with you leading the way, your firm young jaw against the wind.

MAGEE. Susan, have you been smoking the drapes?

SUSAN. (*Rises and crosses U.L.*) Let's tell my parents the idea.

MAGEE. I thought you said they approved?

SUSAN. My mother does. I thought you could tell Dad.

MAGEE. (*Rises and crosses to desk.*) Susan, I can't go through with this.

SUSAN. (*Calling off.*) Mother! Dad! Come quickly, Axel has something to tell you.

MAGEE. Susan, let's discuss this.

SUSAN. (*Crosses to desk.*) Axel, if we stay here it's just a question of time till another bomb comes through the window. . . . You have no right to deny us a chance to save our lives.

MAGEE. (*Crosses to D.S. of table.*) I'm not good at these things. I like a nice quiet evening at home . . .

SUSAN. (*Crosses toward him.*) Axel, we can do it. The two of us . . . together.

MAGEE. Be realistic, Susan—how could you get out of the building?

SUSAN. Well . . . we could dig a tunnel.

MAGEE. Dig a tunnel? Are you kidding? With our knowledge of engineering, we'd probably come up in the stove.

SUSAN. All right, we could sneak out on the back of a laundry truck . . . I saw that in an old prison movie once.

MAGEE. We don't send our laundry out anymore. Your mother does it for the whole Embassy! No, you'd only have a chance, if, say, you were at a party, if you dressed as guests, mingled with the crowd, and left when everybody else leaves.

SUSAN. Axel, that's brilliant!

MAGEE. What is?

SUSAN. Your idea! There's a party here Saturday night for the Sultan—we dress as guests, mingle, and walk right out!

MAGEE. That's the craziest thing I ever heard!

SUSAN. Axel, it's a stroke of genius.

WALTER. (*Enters with* MARION U.L. *They cross* D.L.C.) What's so urgent? What does the failure want to tell us?

SUSAN. Go ahead, Axel—

MAGEE. (*Timid over broaching it.*) Susan . . .

SUSAN. (*Urging tone.*) Axel . . .

MAGEE. (*Squirming before* WALTER, *he finally gets it out.*) Eh—that was an awfully nasty bomb that came through the window before.

WALTER. Did you notice that?

MAGEE. (*Writhing.*) Mr. Hollander, in view of circumstances—after careful consideration, I feel our situation calls for a little action.

WALTER. What kind of action?

MAGEE. Mr. Hollander—supposing you actually were trapped spies? What would you do?

WALTER. I'd deny it and claim to be a caterer—what do you want from me?

MAGEE. You read the papers—what do families do when they're caught behind the Berlin Wall and they want freedom desperately? So desperately—their lives depend on it.

WALTER. What do they do? They escape. They go over walls or through tunnels, they forge passports, they go through roadblocks. . . . It's been wonderful chatting with you, Magee. If you get any other hysterical notions be sure and call me. (*Crosses to* R.C.)

MAGEE. (*Step in.*) Mr. Hollander—it's the only way.

MARION. Escape—what an interesting idea—

WALTER. Magee—you're crazy. Do you know you're crazy? Years of insanity have made you crazy!

SUSAN. (*Step in.*) Why not, Dad? It's better than being trapped here.

MARION. Grouch, will you listen for a minute!

WALTER. (*Crosses to sofa, hands to ears.*) "A foggy day, in London town—"

MAGEE. (*Crosses to him.*) Mr. Hollander. This is a matter of life or death.

WALTER. You picked the wrong person to talk to about an escape! I don't escape from places. That's not my field. I enter and I stay!

MAGEE. It's wrong to reject an idea just because it sounds radical.

WALTER. That's exactly it—it's radical—and when it comes to things like going over walls or forging passports or going through roadblocks, I'm a terrific conservative. I'm the John Birch of the escape world!

MARION. Calm down. Will you please?

WALTER. Marion, did you ever see a man with a hernia running from a tank!?

SUSAN. Dad. You read about it every day. Couples escape—husband escapes—lovers flee tyranny—

WALTER. What you read is—couple *shot* escaping. Husband *shot* escaping. Lovers *killed* fleeing tyranny.

MARION. You're a coward!

WALTER. That's right, Mr. Anthony! If you wanted a hero you should have married Sergeant York!

MARION. Do you want your daughter to grow up here for the rest of her life?

WALTER. I'd rather she grew up here than grew up as an orphan. I'm funny that way, I can tolerate anybody's orphan but my own!

MARION. (*Meaningfully.*) You want your daughter to meet other eligible men, don't you?

WALTER. (*This stops him in his tracks. He considers*

this and then looks at MAGEE, *then more thought, and more scrutiny of* MAGEE. *Finally:*) All right, let me hear it— (*Crosses to* SUSAN.) let me hear this brilliant plot— I haven't had a good laugh in a long time—tell me the plan so I can go ha, ha.

MAGEE. The night after tomorrow there's going to be a reception here—

WALTER. Who's catering it?

MARION. Will you let him finish?

MAGEE. —a big party in honor of the Sultan of Bashir —that night this house will be filled with dignitaries, men and women from all nations, even from this country— you two, and Susan will dress as guests . . . Now then, you'll wait in your room till midnight and when groups of guests leave, you come downstairs, get your coats and go right out with them.

MARION. It'll give you a chance to wear your dark blue mohair.

WALTER. I don't like my dark blue mohair, it itches.

MARION. How can mohair itch? It's a soft fabric.

WALTER. Sue me, it itches!

MARION. Well, you'll have to wear a dark suit, I'm not going to escape if you're not going to dress.

WALTER. We're not going anyplace!

(DROBNEY *comes on* L., *interested by all this talk.*)

MAGEE. Once outside we'll have the Embassy limousine waiting and you're off.

WALTER. And if we did manage to get out of here, what then?

DROBNEY. (*Joining right in.*) The rest is simple! My contacts will see to it you are on your way home within hours.

MAGEE. Mr. Hollander, I appeal to you—for the safety of everyone concerned, we must not procrastinate. Timing is very important.

MARION. We'll see Seth again. I miss him so. By the

way, Walter, I didn't want to mention this because you'd
get upset, but I got a letter from my brother—our apartment was robbed.

WALTER. What!

MARION. Burglars broke in—they stole the portable
TV and all your shirts.

WALTER. (*Crosses below* MAGEE.) I'm cursed. I'm a
cursed caterer. I'm trapped here and somewhere there's
burglars running around with my initials on their cuffs.
(*Sits on sofa, accidentally sitting on bomb, which he
hands to* MAGEE *inadvertently.*)

SUSAN. Dad, let's go home.

DROBNEY. (*Crosses and sits with* WALTER; *appeals to
him.*) Mr. Hollander, I beg you. Magee's plan is a good
one. You can trust him. I know he seems like a bungler,
but he is actually bright and resourceful. He knows exactly what he is doing and you are in good hands.

WALTER. (*Considers* MAGEE *a moment. Although he
doesn't believe it, he figures finally, what the hell, why
not.*) All right, we'll escape.

MAGEE. (*Crosses to* U.R. *of sofa.*) Mr. Hollander, you
have nothing to worry about. I'm in full control.

(*Tosses supposedly dismantled bomb out window and
the Stage is lit up with a huge EXPLOSION. When
it clears,* DROBNEY *stares at* MAGEE *accusingly and
says:*)

DROBNEY. You're a nut!

BLACKOUT

ACT TWO

SCENE 2

Lights up on DROBNEY *facing audience.*

DROBNEY. (D.C.) The next few days were fraught with danger and intrigue. I made several phone calls to enlist the help of some of the most brilliant men in the underground. Unfortunately, they had all been captured. Magee worked around the clock devising an escape so complicated that only three people in the world understood it—and Magee was not one of them. On the morning of the day of escape, they reviewed the plan to make sure it was foolproof.

WALTER. (*Entering wearily* U.R.) It's a rotten plan. It won't work. (*Crossing and sitting sofa.*) Let's call it off.

MARION. (*Enters* U.R.) We're not calling anything off. (*Crosses and sits with* WALTER.)

MAGEE. (*Enters* U.R. *with briefcase, obviously having gone through a lot preparing the* HOLLANDERS. *Crosses to desk, puts down briefcase and crosses to sofa.*) Now then, let's start from the top and go over the entire procedure again. Okay, Mr. Hollander, now who are you?

WALTER. (*Rote.*) I'm John Randall from Washington, D.C. I work in the Department of the Interior. I'm married and I have four children. I was born in Milwaukee, Wisconsin and went to school in California. I majored in agriculture and first entered government under Roosevelt. I drive a Chrysler Imperial; who's gonna ask me those questions?

MAGEE. In the event that you're stopped at any point your answers must be consistent.

WALTER. Ahhh, nobody's gonna believe I'm Sam Randall—

MAGEE *and* MARION. John Randall.

WALTER. John, Sam, I got such a headache.

MAGEE. What are you doing in Europe?

WALTER. (*Slowly, with an acid look at* MARION.) What am I doing in Europe? (*Then.*) I'm making a tour of underdeveloped nations to initiate projects coping with the problems of soil conservation and erosion.

MARION. Very good.

WALTER. Don't very good me—

MARION. And I'm his lovely wife, Carmen. I'm also the former Miss Wisconsin of nineteen thirty-eight.

WALTER. If they believe that, we win the whole cold war. One look at those varicose veins and they'll think I'm smuggling road maps.

MAGEE. Where are you staying in town?

MARION. The Grand Hotel for one week, then we're flying to Malaysia.

MAGEE. All right, now what do you do when you leave here?

WALTER. Uh . . . uh.

MARION. At about midnight, when some of the other guests are leaving we casually say excuse me and leave with the largest group. Our chauffeur then drives us directly to the lobby of the Grand Hotel.

WALTER. Provided we haven't been stopped at the gate, identified, arrested, shot, beaten and tortured.

MARION. At the Grand Hotel we switch cars. A man will come up to me and say, "Those are extremely lovely earrings, my wife has a pair just like them." He will be our driver. We go with him.

MAGEE. Correct.

WALTER. What if a stranger happens to like her earrings? We'll wind up following him to Lapland.

MAGEE. What happens when he takes you to the railroad station?

WALTER. He takes us to the railroad station and a guy comes up to us, presumably not suspicious-looking, who says to me, "The grass is green," which for my money, he might as well wear a neon sign saying, "I am a spy."

MAGEE. And what do you do?

WALTER. We get on the train with him, heading for

Istanbul. (*Rises and crosses* R.C.) Another first in my life, I need Istanbul like the plague. With my fear of Turks.

MAGEE. But you don't get to Istanbul.

MARION. (*Rises.*) Half way there we jump off the train.

WALTER. Oh, I'm really looking forward to that. It's been so long since I've jumped off a moving train.

MAGEE. Your contact will assist you in all these maneuvers.

MARION. (*Crosses to him.*) What are you so worried about?

WALTER. We'll wait and see how well you jump. You practically break a leg finding a seat in the movies.

MARION. After leaving the train, we're met by a man driving a wagon load of hay.

MAGEE. Correct.

MARION. We dress up as peasants, get up on the wagon and go with him.

WALTER. It has to be hay, right. I got the worst hay fever in America. Must be hay.

MARION. He takes us to the seashore where we're picked up by a submarine. Isn't it thrilling, Walter?

WALTER. A submarine? Yesterday it was a plane.

MAGEE. (*Crosses to desk.*) It had to be changed. Security precautions.

WALTER. Thanks for telling me, I would have spent all day looking for wings.

MAGEE. Now then, here's some local currency—

WALTER. (*Crosses to* L.C. *chair.*) No, it's all right, I got money. You get the next one.

MARION. Take it, Walter. You only have traveller's checks.

WALTER. They're good anywhere.

MARION. (*Crosses to him.*) You're gonna stop in the middle of a chase through an alley and start signing traveller's checks?

WALTER. What do you mean chasing through alleys?

You said this was going to be simple. I can't run. I'm an old man with orthopedic shoes. (*Sits* L.C. *chair.*)

MAGEE. (*Crosses with briefcase, hands* WALTER *money.*) I suggest you take this money. (WALTER *takes it.*) Incidentally, have you ever shot a pistol? (*Gets pistol from briefcase.*)

WALTER. Shot a pistol? How often in the catering business is there a gun fight?

MAGEE. (*Handing it to* WALTER.) It's very simple. It can't fire unless you release this safety catch. Then just squeeze the trigger.

WALTER. (*Rises. Intrigued by it.*) It's a beauty.

(MAGEE *crosses* R. *of desk.*)

MARION. I don't think you should carry a gun.

WALTER. Why not?

MARION. They're dangerous.

WALTER. They're not dangerous.

MARION. But you don't know how to use one.

WALTER. Don't tell me, I can use a gun.

MARION. When did you ever use a gun?

WALTER. Plenty of times, don't worry—

MARION. When?

WALTER. I want to carry it.

MARION. (*Crosses to desk.*) I don't want you to carry a gun.

WALTER. (*Crosses toward her.*) Why can't I carry a gun? I want a gun. What's wrong? Why can't I have a gun?

MARION. I'm not going if you carry a gun.

MAGEE. Maybe Mrs. Hollander has a point. I'm being overcautious. There won't be any need for it.

WALTER. (*To* MARION.) Why do you have to take the fun out of everything we do?

MARION. All right, you can carry it, but keep it unloaded.

MAGEE. (*Crosses to* R. *door.*) You'd always have the

time to load it. But you won't need it— I've got every angle figured. (*Exits* R.)

WALTER. (*A la Sam Spade.*) You can never tell when this little piece of tin can spell the difference . . .

MARION. (*Crosses to sofa. Tensely.*) Well . . . this is it.

WALTER. Don't worry, it'll be a cinch.

MARION. You got very confident all of a sudden.

WALTER. Ah, everybody makes a big deal out of nothing.

MARION. (*Beginning to tear.*) You think so?

WALTER. Sure, the whole thing'll be over in two hours. It won't be any worse an ordeal than your sister's wedding.

MARION. (*Sits sofa. Crying a bit now.*) You think so?

WALTER. What are you crying about? . . . She's crying already.

MARION. (*More crying.*) I'm sorry.

WALTER. (*Crosses* U.S. *of sofa.*) Can't you go any place without crying? Every time we make plans you have to get upset. That's why I never want to go any place. And that's why I was not keen on escaping. Because I knew you'd make it into a federal case. What's the matter? (*Crosses to* R. *of sofa.*)

MARION. I don't know.

WALTER. What do you mean, you don't know? How can you not know what you're crying about? Does something hurt you?

MARION. (*Crying.*) I'm afraid—

WALTER. (*Crosses* D.R. *of sofa.*) Aha, you're not such a big shot any more. You talk a good game . . . stop crying . . . everything's gonna be all right— (*Crosses and sits with her.*) . . . come on . . . this is going to be simple as pie . . there's nothing to be worried about . . . What's the worst thing that could happen? We'll get caught? Big deal . . . they'll try us and torture us? So what? We bite down on those cyanide capsules . . . (MARION *lets out a big wail.*) stop crying . . . leave everything to me, will you please do that? (*An arm around her.*) Will you trust me? . . . I know what I'm doing . . . I'll take care of us, don't worry . . . you think I'm gonna let anybody hurt you? You remember when we were first married, a soldier whistled at you at Palisades Amusement Park, I gave him a sock in the mouth?

MARION. (*Reminiscing.*) Yeah, he was a little tiny thing—

WALTER. You were so beautiful in your puce Aztec shawl . . .

MARION. And you with that dark blue dress suit, with the white socks and the saddle shoes . . .

WALTER. (*Arm down.*) That was doctor's orders, I had a foot infection.

MARION. Walter, will you protect me?

WALTER. Have I ever let you down? . . . Ever? Did I stand by you right from the start when my mother despised you? Did I hold your hand through two pregnancies, four false alarms, and a very complicated oral prophylaxis? Now come on . . . have a little faith in me . . . I'll see that we come out right side up.

MARION. Walter . . . I've been such a terrible wife . . .

WALTER. Not at all . . . I'm not easy to live with. You'd be amazed but a lot of women would find me unpleasant.

MARION. No . . .

WALTER. Sure . . . Now come on, go upstairs and rest for a while and then you ought to start getting ready. (BOTH *rise.*)

MARION. I'm wearing my new dress.

WALTER. You better bring a pair of sneakers . . .

MARION. Wally . . . (*They embrace.*)

WALTER. (*Breaks it.*) You haven't called me that since the Harvest Moon Ball and even then I said if you ever did, I'd break your neck—

MARION. (*Crosses to* U.L. *arch.*) I'm going, I'm going. (*She exits up stairs.*)

WALTER. (*Calling after her.*) I'm gonna read my paper. I'll see you later. And don't worry . . . you're dealing with a guy who can handle himself . . . (*Removes revolver, tries twirling it, puts it in his belt—walks across Stage like a constipated gun fighter ready to draw against his foe.*)

KILROY. (*Enters R. and crosses D.R.C.*) Mr. Hollander—

(WALTER *turns rapidly, drawing his pistol which goes off and nails* KILROY *in the leg.* KILROY *dances on one foot and there is an immediate:*)

BLACKOUT

ACT TWO

SCENE 3

Lights up on party for SULTAN. *The night is nearly over and only a few* GUESTS *remain. The* SULTAN *and his* WIFE *are present, drinking heavily. MUSIC, swinging, fills the background.*

MAGEE. (*Nervously looking to stairway, awaiting the* HOLLANDERS' *entrance, crosses to* SULTAN.) Ah, there you are, Your Majesty. Why don't you come inside and join the party? Did you enjoy being guest of honor?

SULTAN. (*Quite tipsy.*) Ah, Mr. Magee—there is nothing better to cement wounded pride than bourbon.

MAGEE. (*Wants to get him out of room.*) Er, yes—there's plenty of bourbon inside.

SULTAN. Whatever happened to the American from New Jersey? The mongrel.

MAGEE. He couldn't come but he sends his apologies and best wishes. I'm delighted you consented to give us the opportunity to honor you, Your Majesty. You know how my father feels about you.

SULTAN. Where is your father?

MAGEE. He meant to get back for the party. But his plane was delayed. He'll probably come after everyone is gone.

(SULTAN *and* WIFE *exit* U.R.C. *to next room, unsteady.* DROBNEY *enters* U.L. *suspiciously, cases room, head-beckons* MAGEE *to come to him* D.L.C., *which* MAGEE *does, sensing something's up.*)

DROBNEY. (*Gets out cards.*) Pick a card.

MAGEE. Not now, Father!

DROBNEY. (*Forcing deck on him.*) Go ahead—take one.

MAGEE. I'm not in the mood for magic.

DROBNEY. There's a message written on the two of spades.

MAGEE. You can tell me the message, Father. No one will hear.

(DROBNEY *tries to find the two of spades in a deck of obviously all two of spades. Finally he gets it and reads:*)

DROBNEY. "The Hollanders are ready."

MAGEE. That's the message?

(DROBNEY *goes off* L.)

SUSAN. (*Comes downstairs dressed as guest at the reception. Crosses to desk.*) Axel.

MAGEE. (*Crosses to* SUSAN.) Where are your parents?

SUSAN. They're coming. My father's having trouble getting his holster on.

MAGEE. The house is crawling with trouble. Krojack is here. If I tried to keep anyone away it would look suspicious. You better move fast. The coast is clear.

SUSAN. Goodbye, Axel. I'll speak to you in a few days.

MAGEE. We have some future plans to discuss.

(*And she exits toward front hallway.* WALTER *and* MARION *come downstairs, then suddenly reverse their tracks and run back up. We see why as the* SULTAN *crosses near bottom of stairway. Now, with* SULTAN *gone, they come down again and head straight for front door and suddenly we see them turn in horror and head back toward stairs to go up again. We see* KROJACK *crossing toward them and he is the reason they turned, but now the path to the staircase is no good because the* SULTAN *is crossing back. The scene now is that* KROJACK *is walking toward the* SULTAN *with the* HOLLANDERS *in the middle. This all happens Upstage, and for a moment they are all hidden behind a center panel. After a second,* KROJACK *emerges, still heading in his direction and the* SULTAN *emerges still heading in his. They cross off. Finally, the* HOLLANDERS *emerge.*)

MARION. Walter, you haven't hugged and kissed me like that in twenty-five years.

WALTER. That was you? What are we gonna do?

MARION. Try and appear casual.

WALTER. (*Crosses to* U.S. *of table.*) I am appearing casual.

MARION. You know, Walter, you can tell you're carrying a gun.

WALTER. Get out of here, you can not.

MARION. (*Crosses to him.*) Walter, there's a big bulge under your shoulder.

WALTER. It's the way I'm built.

MARION. It's not the way you're built. You don't have a handle.

WALTER. (*Crosses to* D.S. *of* L.C. *chair.*) Leave me alone.

MARION. (*To him.*) Put it upstairs.

WALTER. We need it.

MARION. We don't need it. You shot Mr. Kilroy today; it's dangerous.

WALTER. It went off accidentally.

MARION. Walter, people are staring at your bulge.

WALTER. (*Hands on ears, he crosses to get away from her and bumps into a* GUEST.) "A foggy day, in London town . . ."

KASNAR. We have not met, have we?

WALTER. (*Lapsing into his speech.*) I'm John Randall from Washington, D.C. I work in the Department of the Interior, I'm married and I have four children. I was born in Milwaukee, Wisconsin and went to school in California. I majored in agriculture and first entered Government under Roosevelt . . . I drive a Chrysler Imperial. I'm John Randall . . .

MARION. (*Follows story by rote, then comes in with:*) And I am his lovely wife, Carmen.

KASNAR. How do you do? Yanis Kasnar, and this is the Countess Wilhamena Bordoni.

COUNTESS. Charmed.

MARION. (*Pinching him.*) Say hello to the Countess, darling.

WALTER. (*Nervously.*) Hello, darling.

KASNAR. (*Holding up his glass.*) This wine is extraordinary. Have you tasted it?

COUNTESS. Uhmmm . . . exquisite.

(WALTER *takes* KASNAR'S *glass, drains it in one gulp. Hands glass back.*)

KASNAR. Yes, rather diffident and ephemeral, wouldn't you say, Mr. Randall?

WALTER. (*Squirms a moment, then:*) Hmm, the bouquet is subtly demure and yet the flavor is playfully articulate. (*Then aside to* MARION.) Esquire Magazine.

KASNAR. How long have you been here?

MARION. (*She and* WALTER *talk simultaneously.*) Two weeks.

WALTER. Just a few days.

MARION. A few days.

WALTER. Two weeks. We're at the big hotel . . .

MARION. We're staying at the Grand Hotel . . .

WALTER. I don't care for it . . .

MARION. It's beautiful . . . Well, we really must be going, it's late. Come, Walter.

KASNAR. Walter?

WALTER. (*With a nudge.*) How amusing. My own wife forgets I'm Sam Randall.

KASNAR. Sam?

MARION. (*Correcting* WALTER.) John.

WALTER. John, Sam, Walter—my real name was Randall John Sam but everyone in Washington confused it with Lyndon Johnson—John Sam, Johnson—I kept getting all his meat bills and phone messages.

KASNAR. How interesting.

WALTER. (*To* MARION.) Let's go. We're due in Afghanistan.

MARION. Tunisia.

WALTER. Afghanistan, Tunisia . . . Come on, Marion.

COUNTESS. Marion?

MARION. I'm his lovely wife, Carmen.

(*The* COUNTESS *drops her fan.* WALTER *goes to pick it up.* KASNAR *crosses to desk and puts glass down.*)

WALTER. Allow me . . . OH! (*His pistol falls to floor as he goes to pick up fan. There is a tense moment.* EVERYONE *stares. He writhes. Finally he says:*) My— my cigarette lighter.

KASNAR. (*Crosses to* L. *of* WALTER. *An unlit cigarette in his mouth.*) May I have a light?

(*Trapped,* WALTER *fakes trying to light cigarette with his gun and* MARION *stands back anticipating a shot. Finally, when nothing happens:*)

WALTER. Damn Zippos, never work.

KASNAR. No matter. Well, we must be going. The

party is about over and I hate to be the last to leave. (*Exits* U.R. *with* COUNTESS, *leaving* WALTER *and* MARION *alone.*)

MARION. Lucky those Zippos never work.

WALTER. C'mon, Marion.

(*They start off* U.R. *when* KROJACK *enters* U.L.)

KROJACK. (*Crosses to* D.S. *of desk.*) So, my friends, we meet again.

WALTER. (*Crosses toward him.*) What'd you do, roll a drunk and steal his invitation?

KROJACK. You're all dressed up. Are you going someplace?

DROBNEY. (*Enters urgently* U.L.) Krojack—telephone call for you—urgent. Why don't you take it in my room? it's quiet up there. Hurry—they're holding.

KROJACK. (*Wavers, then decides it might be 'important.*) I will deal with you later. (*He goes off with* DROBNEY *up stairs and after he's off,* MARION *and* WALTER *leave* U.R. *for front door.*)

MAGEE. (*Enters* L., *crosses to* D.S. *of desk.*) Where are they?

BURNS. (*Enters* U.R. *and crosses to* MAGEE.) They've gone. Once they're past the police at the gate the rest is not hard.

MAGEE. If we don't hear anything in the next two minutes we can assume they've made it.

BURNS. (*Tensely imagining.*) By now they're going down the front steps. Now they're going to the car—slowly—deliberately.

MAGEE. Now they're up to the gate. They're going through all together. The police have no reason to stop them. (DROBNEY *runs downstairs and crosses off* L. KROJACK *follows after him in pursuit, only he's wearing a straitjacket.*) I wonder if this is happening in any other embassy.

(*Suddenly from outside we hear GUNSHOTS and COM-MOTION.*)

BURNS. What is that?

SUSAN. (*Entering* U.L., *crossing to* MAGEE.) Oh, Axel—it's terrible.

MARION. (*Entering, pale,* U.L., *crosses* D.R.C.) Walter, how could you do it?

WALTER. (*Entering with smoking revolver* U.L., *crosses* D.R.C.) It was dark—I couldn't see anything.

(*Enter* AMBASSADOR MAGEE U.L., *shot in the leg, and furious.*)

MAGEE. *DAD!*

BLACKOUT

ACT TWO

SCENE 4

Lights up on next morning. AMBASSADOR MAGEE *in wheelchair, is furious with* AXEL, *who pushes chair* D.C.

AMBASSADOR. How could you do it? How could you attempt an escape?

MAGEE. Dad, the situation called for something bold. If it had worked, we'd all be heroes.

AMBASSADOR. But it failed, as everything you do fails. Picketing, riots, bombs—this never happened in my Embassy before. And this morning a devout priest produced a seven of spades from my ear.

MAGEE. Father Drobney was trying to cheer you up, sir.

AMBASSADOR. I'll get you for this, Axel—I'll find a way—I promise.

SUSAN. (*Enters* L.) Excuse me.

AMBASSADOR. I'm finished with him, Miss Hollander. (*To* MAGEE.) By the way, your mother called. She wants you to mail her your birth certificate. Through two world wars without a scratch only to be shot by a caterer. (*And he wheels himself off* U.L.)

SUSAN. (*Crosses to* MAGEE.) Axel, I'm sorry. It's all our fault.

MAGEE. No, it isn't. But now they've doubled the guard outside.

WALTER. (*Enters with* MARION U.L. BOTH *cross* D.L.C.) Well, Magee, it was a nice try. Unfortunately, I shot the boss, but those are the breaks.

MARION. I guess we're here for good now.

MAGEE. I got you into this and I promise I'll get you out.

WALTER. Well, I'm ready, willing and able to try anything. I feel I've been toughened up by our first attempt. Now that I've actually drawn blood. True, it was your father's—

(*Sound of MOAN from other room.*)

MAGEE. What was that?

SUSAN. (*Goes and peeks into other room.*) It's the Sultan of Bashir and his wife, and are they unconscious!

(MAGEE *goes to take a look.*)

WALTER. Serves 'em right. They drank up enough alcohol last night to rub down the Green Bay Packers.

MARION. I better call Barney Silverman. He's probably still at Montauk Point with the station wagon waiting for us to surface.

MAGEE. (*Returning with* BURNS U.R., *crosses to* R. *door*. BURNS *follows*.) Mr. Burns, the Sultan and his wife have had a little too much party. You better put them to bed. If you have any trouble moving the Sultan, there's a dolly downstairs. Find some pajamas for them—pajamas—pajamas—pajamas— (*An idea has hit* MAGEE *and he sizes up* WALTER. BURNS *exits.*)

WALTER. Magee, why are you looking at me like that and repeating the word pajamas?

MAGEE. (*Crosses to* U.L. *arch.*) I'll bet it would work.

SUSAN. Axel, what are you thinking?

MAGEE. (*Yells off.*) Father Drobney, come here quickly. (*Crosses to sofa.*)

WALTER. Magee, if there's something going through that mind of yours besides the usual cattle stampede, you want to tell us.

MAGEE. (*Holds pillow to* WALTER'S *stomach.*) Size is about right. (*Crosses to* SUSAN.)

SUSAN. Axel, I know what you're thinking, but there's two of them and three of us.

MAGEE. No one saw them leave last night, so if they leave now it'll look perfectly natural. Except underneath those royal robes will not be His Majesty at all but the phantom caterer!

WALTER. It sounds great! It won't work—but it sounds great!

MARION. It's just crazy enough to work.

MAGEE. You two change quickly. (*Hustles* WALTER *and* MARION *into room with unconscious Sultan.*)

SUSAN. What about me?

MAGEE. I'll come to you. Mr. Burns, please assist them. (*Closes door on all of them.*)

SUSAN. Axel, are you sure you know what you're doing?

MAGEE. (*Takes* SUSAN D.R.C.) Susan, for the first time since this whole thing started I feel in complete control. This is going to work.

DROBNEY. (*Enters* U.L. *and crosses* D.L. *of desk.*) You called?

MAGEE. Yes, Father. Are your contacts still ready to go on a moment's notice?

DROBNEY. (*Crosses to* U.S. *of desk.*) Yes, I'm sure.

MAGEE. Then alert them quickly.

(DROBNEY *quickly gets on phone.*)

SUSAN. Axel. This is so thrilling. You're actually having an idea.

MAGEE. Susan. Every now and then fate comes along, takes a man by the hand and enables him to build a mountain.

SUSAN. (*Thrilled.*) Oh, Axel! How corny.

MAGEE. (*Pulls* SUSAN D.R.) Susan. I'm going to get you all home safely—right now.

DROBNEY. (*Into phone, significantly.*) The storm we were expecting will be a little late. I think the same precautions are in order.

MAGEE. Susan. Have I told you lately that I love you?

SUSAN. No. But if you want to I think we can work something out.

DROBNEY. Ready to go?

WALTER. (*Enters* R. *with* MARION *dressed as* SULTAN *and* WIFE. *They cross* D.L.) His suit itches.

MARION. How can it itch? It's silk.

WALTER. I've explained a thousand times about my skin. My dermatologist says I've got the thighs of a princess.

DROBNEY. (*Crosses toward* WALTER.) Everything is ready. Go immediately. God bless you.

MAGEE. Try to be as casual and confident as you can and if anyone talks to you, mutter something about Allah.

DROBNEY. The driver will take you to the Grand Hotel. From there on our plan will be precisely the same.

MARION. What about Susan?

MAGEE. She's going to walk out with me in a little while under the protection of full diplomatic immunity.

SUSAN. How?

MAGEE. As the wife of a foreign diplomat, you get that privilege.

WALTER. (*Crosses* D.R.) Wife? You and her?

MAGEE. Why not? We're United States citizens in United States territory. We're over twenty-one and Father Drobney is a priest. It's perfect.

SUSAN. (*Thrilled.*) Oh, Axel.

MARION. (*Hugging* SUSAN.) My Susan a bride! This is the happiest day of my life. I only wish your father were alive to see it.

WALTER. I am alive. I'm right here.

MARION. (*Crosses to* WALTER.) Oh, I'm sorry, dear— I got carried away.

SUSAN. Axel, it's brilliant!

WALTER. (*Crosses to* MAGEE.) What if she doesn't want to marry you?

SUSAN. I do—I do.

WALTER. You do? (*To* MAGEE.) May Allah twist your nose off.

MAGEE. We've got to act fast.

(SUSAN *kisses* MARION, *then* WALTER.)

MARION. (*To* SUSAN.) While we're aboard the submarine, you wire us your silverware pattern.

WALTER. (*To* MAGEE.) May all the sands of the desert fill your navel.

SUSAN. See you in Newark in a few days.

MAGEE. Hurry—please.

WALTER. Come on, Marion—I better get home and register his name at the unemployment insurance office.

MARION. (*To* SUSAN.) On the way home I'll stop at the drugstore and send you a bottle of those pills.

MAGEE. (*Proudly.*) Mr. Hollander. Remember, sir, you're not losing a daughter—you're gaining a son.

WALTER. May all the camels in Egypt—ah, forget it.

(*And he and* MARION *exit* U.R.)

DROBNEY. (*Crosses* D.R.C. *Stepping forward and ad-*

dressing audience as MAGEE *and* SUSAN *kiss and freeze.*)
Incidentally, the Hollanders made it safely to Newark. I
married Susan and Magee. And Ambassador Magee is
still running for Governor without the Sultan's help. And
just to be sure no one causes any trouble he sent Magee
five thousand miles away to Bolivia, where for the first
time in two hundred years that country had a plague of
locusts. (*To* MAGEE *and* SUSAN.) *Pick* a card—go ahead
—pick a card.

(*MUSIC up.*)

CURTAIN

PROPERTY PLOT

On Desk:
Files, envelopes, document, note pad, pencil, telephone

On Table:
Decanter, 3 glasses, cigarette box, ash-tray

On Cabinet:
Flowers

Off Right:
Wheelchair with blanket (Ambassador)
Bomb (2-1)
Gun (blanks)
Cover gun (blanks)
Briefcase with gun (loaded), money (Magee)
Tommy gun (Guard)
Recorder (Krojack)
Folder (Magee)
Dummy gun (Krojack)*
Pad and pencil (Kilroy)
Cot with blankets and sheets (Kilroy and Burns)
Flowers (2-3)
3 pairs socks (1-3)

Off Left:
3 glasses wine (Kasnar, Countess, Novotny)
2 old fashioned drinks (Sultan, Sultan's Wife)
Hamper with dove in cage, magic cane, magic light bulb,
   cylinder, box (Drobney)
Straight jacket (Drobney)
2 packages (Magee and Susan)
1 suitcase (Walter)
5 suitcases (Marion)
1 suitcase (Susan)
Drink (Susan)
Rabbit (Chef)

* Double

Duster (Marion)
Ironing board with iron and shirt (1-3)
Basket with clothes, 2 shirts on top (1-3)
Bowl flowers (2-3)
Business card (Walter)
Book (Marion)
Cigarette case with cigarettes (Kasnar)
Deck of cards (Drobney)
Camera (Walter)
Pad and pencil (Walter)
Toothbrush, toothpaste, razor, shaving cream (Walter)
2 letters (Walter)
Dummy gun and holster (Walter)

PROP CUES

ACT 1—*Scene 1*
Take machine guns on stage right and lock up

ACT 1—*Scene 2*

Strike:
  Cot (s.L.)

ACT 1—*Scene 2* to ACT 1—*Scene 3*

Set:
  Laundry basket
  Ironing board
  Socks

Strike:
  Magic to under stairs

ACT 1—*Scene 3*
Put bird back

Set:
  Cloth bag and glass at top of stairs, luggage down stage (s.L.)

INTERMISSION

Re-rig table
Clear desk
Strike luggage, flowers, decanter and glasses

ACT 2—*Scene 1*
8 gun shots

ACT 2—*Scene 2* to ACT 2—*Scene 3*

Set:
  Flowers on desk
  Flowers on phono
Close window

ACT 2—*Scene 3*
Lock up guns
Clean glasses
Cover desk at end of show

COSTUME PLOT

NOTE:

MARION's handbag should be same throughout except in Act 2—Scene 3.

DROBNEY—same throughout.

KILROY—same throughout with additions as indicated.

ACT 1—*Scene 1*

WALTER—loud print short-sleeved shirt worn outside pants, beige pants, dark green felt "porky" hat with feather, white socks, sandals

MAGEE—black suit with vest, white shirt, tie, black shoes

MARION—white coat, dark lavender dress, light lavender scarf, black hand-bag, black shoes, hairpiece

SUSAN—tangerine suit, beige blouse, beige shoes, straw bag

AMBASSADOR—dark-striped suit with vest, white shirt, tie, black shoes

DROBNEY—cassock, priest's collar on bib, black shoes

KILROY—walking suit (striped pants, black jacket, pearl grey vest), white shirt, striped tie, black shoes

KROJACK—grey striped suit, white shirt, tie, black shoes

GUARD—Uniform with buster brown belt, matching hat

BURNS—grey suit, white shirt, black tie, black shoes

ACT 1—*Scene 2*

WALTER—same as ACT 1—*Scene 1*, no hat

MAGEE—same as ACT 1—*Scene 1*

MARION—same as ACT 1—*Scene 1*, no coat

SUSAN—same at ACT 1—*Scene 1*, no bag

BURNS—same as ACT 1—*Scene 1*

CHEF—white jacket, white pants, white scarf

ACT 1—*Scene 3*

WALTER—maroon bathrobe, brown slippers

MARION—dark blue print kimono, light blue slippers, same as

83

ACT 1—*Scene 2,* black bag

SUSAN—navy blue dress, beige shoes, orange bloomers

BURNS—same as ACT 1—*Scene 2*

SULTAN—maroon toga, white robe, white and black striped head shawl; red, black and gold head-band, black shoes, medallion on chain

WIFE—maroon robe, maroon head-gear adorned with black and gold coins and white veil, black slippers

ACT 1—*Scene 4*

WALTER—dark suit, white shirt, tie, hat, same as ACT 1—*Scene 1,* black shoes

MAGEE—same as ACT 1—*Scene 3*

MARION—white coat, same at ACT 1—*Scene 1,* pink dress, beige shoes, black bag, black gloves

SUSAN—orange and pink striped coat, beige shoes

CHEF—same as ACT 1—*Scene 2*

BURNS—same as ACT 1—*Scene 3*

KROJACK—same as ACT 1—*Scene 1*

ACT 2—*Scene 1*

WALTER—maroon jacket, black pants, white shirt, tie, black shoes

MAGEE—dark grey suit, tie, white shirt, black shoes

MARION—paisley full length blue robe, blue slippers same as ACT 1—*Scene 3,* black bag

SUSAN—white sleeveless slip dress, beige shoes, long beads

KILROY—add sling

BURNS—grey suit, black tie, white shirt, black shoes

ACT 2—*Scene 2*

WALTER—same as ACT 2—*Scene 1,* change to dark grey jacket

MAGEE—same as ACT 2—*Scene 1,* no jacket, open tie

MARION—dark rose suit, black bag, black shoes

KILROY—add head bandage

ACT 2—*Scene 3*

WALTER—dark blue suit, white shirt, tie, black shoes

MAGEE—dark blue suit, white shirt, tie, black shoes

SUSAN—tangerine evening gown, tangerine shoes, tangerine stole

MARION—white brocade evening coat, white evening purse, white gloves, earrings, white shoes

KROJACK—same as in ACT 1—*Scene 4*

BURNS—tuxedo

SULTAN—same as in ACT 1—*Scene 3*

WIFE—same as in ACT 1—*Scene 3*

AMBASSADOR—dark suit (1 trouser leg torn below knee), white shirt, tie, black shoes

KASNAR—tuxedo

COUNTESS—jade green evening gown, green fan, green earrings, green shoes, long white gloves

NOVOTNY—tuxedo

ACT 2—*Scene 4*

WALTER—same as ACT 2—*Scene 3*, change to maroon jacket

MAGEE—same as ACT 2—*Scene 3*, remove jacket

MARION—same as ACT 1—*Scene 2*, no hairpiece

SUSAN—light blue jumper dress, beige shoes

AMBASSADOR—same as ACT 2—*Scene 3*, remove jacket—put on green plaid bathrobe

BURNS—grey suit, white shirt, black tie, black shoes

WALTER and MARION—change into duplicates of Sultan and Wife costumes

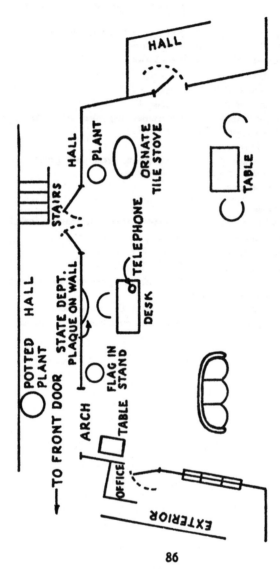

SCENE DESIGN
"DON'T DRINK THE WATER"

Also By Woody Allen...

Death

Death Knocks

God

The Floating Light Bulb

Play it Again, Sam